In 2012 Marvin Dixon had the idea for a crime thriller based in the City of London. Drawn from some of his own experiences in the world of financial services, *Settlement* became his debut novel. Now retired and living in West Yorkshire, writing is his passion.

Marvin Dixon

Settlement

AUSTIN MACAULEY PUBLISHERS™
LONDON • CAMBRIDGE • NEW YORK • SHARJAH

A CIP catalogue record for this title is available from the British Library.

ISBN 9781528930031 (Paperback)
ISBN 9781528930048 (Hardback)
ISBN 9781528966115 (ePub e-book)

www.austinmacauley.com

First Published (2019)
Austin Macauley Publishers Ltd
25 Canada Square
Canary Wharf
London
E14 5LQ

Special thanks to Kat who provided the 'kick in the butt' to get this book written. Also to Ange, John, Steve, Luciano and Bill for their feedback, guidance and support which was invaluable in getting the job done.

Foreword

This is a work of fiction which is set with a backdrop of the financial services industry and specifically life settlement funds. Life settlement funds are genuine investment vehicles and from time to time have been the subject of interest to the UK regulatory authorities.

I have no strong views on the validity of these investments, but they do provide an interesting concept that is the central tenet of this story.

I have taken various liberties with some of the technical aspects of the workings within the fund management world, but remember, this is a work of fiction and the old adage goes that you should never let the truth get in the way of a good story.

Any similarities to anyone living or dead are purely coincidental. I hope you enjoy my tale and remember, be very careful where to invest your hard-earned money. All investments carry a degree of risk, but some are more deadly than others.

Marvin Dixon, West Yorkshire June 2018

Chapter 1

Today was the one day in the year when Henry Gray would get home and Carol would actually smile. He would also get a hug and a kiss, and she would tell him how proud she was. He'd been an analyst at Chartered Asset Management for two years and since his promotion back in 2009, his annual bonus had increased to an amount which got him a 'well done you' from Carol.

They were a relatively small team at CAM, two fund managers, Mike and Tim, supported by himself and Joe, the other analyst and four admin staff of varying ability. They ran two funds which were growing year on year and Mike and Tim returned decent growth. Henry acknowledged they did a decent job but was convinced he could do better. When he kept things "ticking over" when they were on holiday or ill, he could see the opportunities they were missing. OK, some were outside the risk profile of the fund, but that could be changed. If only they'd give him a chance, then maybe Carol would start respecting him like she used to when they'd first met.

As expected, John Harding, the CEO, started calling staff into his office late in the afternoon. They went in order of seniority to be told how much this year's bonus would be. There was no set formula; Harding simply dished out the money as he saw fit, but Mike and Tim always got the lion's share of the available pot. Henry didn't have an issue with this, after all it was them who mainly drove the profitability of the business.

Harding gave Henry his full-on smile. 'Now then Henry, another excellent year and I really want to thank you for all your hard work,' Henry smiled back and nodded a thank you. Harding's smile dimmed slightly as he went on. 'However, while everyone is getting a bonus similar to last year, we need to invest in our IT systems to set us up for the challenges ahead.' He paused, looking as if he expected Henry to say something. Henry wondered what was coming and just kept looking at Harding. After an uncomfortable pause, Harding continued, 'Anyway, your bonus is £4,000; I know it's a bit less than last year, but I've got to consider the overall business. You do great work, Henry, and I really don't want to lose you.'

Random thoughts went through his mind: *what will Carol say; why is he saying he doesn't want to lose me; what should I say next...* He quickly gathered his composure and blurted out the first thing that came into his head. 'I really want to be a fund manager. I've got all the qualifications, so what else do I have to do to make it happen?' Harding regained his smile; he was back on easier ground. 'Of course, I understand your ambition Henry, and if anything changes with Mike or Tim, you'd certainly be in the frame.'

Back in the office everyone was discussing the next social outing. After work on paydays they would go to Hung, Drawn and Quartered on Great Tower Street, but at bonus time they'd usually plan a trip out somewhere. Depending on what was decided, not everyone would go and by the time Henry returned to his desk, there was already a general consensus for rock climbing down in Somerset. They'd been there a couple of years ago and the outdoor centre offered several activities, so there were alternatives for the non-climbers. Henry grunted his assent for Tim to make the arrangements for a weekend in April as he shut down his computer and headed home to face Carol's wrath.

'What do you mean only £4,000?' Carol screamed at him. 'That's not much more than £2,000 after tax, and I've got a new three-piece suite on order!' Henry knew better than to try and have a sensible conversation, so interjected where he could, but 'investing in infrastructure', 'I told him I want a promotion', 'it'll be better next year', was all he could manage. He knew she'd run out of steam eventually and then, providing he got enough Sauvignon Blanc down her, he could get things back on an even keel.

Things settled down over the weekend, and when Carol went off to her shift at the hospital on Sunday morning, Henry lay in bed thinking about how he could change his dull, unfulfilled and lonely existence. He didn't really consider leaving Carol; he still loved her, despite her delusions of grandeur, she kept a tidy house and cared for him in her own way. He resented the fact she kept her inheritance stashed away in some secret account and wouldn't use it to help out when they needed something, like the suite that was coming next week or replacing his ten-year-old Hyundai, which was breaking down with increasing frequency. She assured him it was there for emergencies without elaborating on what qualified as an emergency. His mind turned to work and how he could realise his dream of becoming a fund manager. The answer was obvious; he would need to leave CAM as Mike and Tim didn't look like going anywhere anytime soon, so he decided to take matters into his own hands and speak to some recruiters. There was also the rock-climbing trip to look forward to, so feeling things weren't too bad after all, he went downstairs to check the list of jobs that Carol was certain to have left him.

A few weeks later, as the climbing weekend approached, he was feeling rather pleased with himself. He'd tidied up his CV and met a couple of recruitment agencies who had made positive noises about his experience and qualifications and getting him some interviews. Carol had responded well to his proactivity, even telling him to have a good time on the trip.

Of the five heading over to Paddington for the 17:10 to Bristol, Henry was recognised as the most accomplished climber. Not an expert by any means, but the others looked to him to check their equipment, show them the right knots and generally lead the party. Tim was also a decent climber, but this was just the second time for Mike, although he did have the confidence of being 'an expert' in just about every sport he tried. Paul and James, the two admin guys, had only climbed indoors.

They picked up the minibus at Temple Meads for the 30-minute drive to the hotel near Avon Gorge. They checked-in just before seven thirty, dumped their gear and headed straight to the pub over the road. Henry wasn't much of a drinker, so after a pint and a half with his fish and chips, he went back to the hotel leaving the others who seemed settled in for the night. Back in his room, he unpacked his equipment, a selection from what he'd acquired over the years, and went through the ritual of checking everything meticulously. The rest of the guys were hiring theirs from the outdoor centre.

Saturday morning's breakfast was a quiet affair; the guys had staggered back just after closing time. Copious amounts of coffee and orange juice were consumed, but only Henry had a cooked breakfast.

He was pleased to get everyone to the first climb just ten minutes later than he'd planned. The climbs all had pre-set routes with anchor points all the way. Pothole Crag was a beginner's climb, which he hoped would give everyone confidence. It was a 20-metre ascent, and despite the fuzzy heads, everyone coped well.

There was direct correlation between hangovers disappearing and the level of banter, particularly from Mike, who despite his inexperience, proved annoyingly proficient. Henry had taken years to achieve a decent level of confidence.

'Come on Henry, can't we do something a bit more challenging this afternoon,' said Mike as they ate the soup and sandwiches the hotel had provided for their lunch. 'We should be thrill-seeking, not pottering up nursery slopes my old nan could climb!' This brought a collective chorus of agreement, although Henry detected some nervous looks. Mike noticed this as well and went on, 'Guys, look, this is only my second time and I'm happy to give an unassisted climb a go, so how about it?'

'It wouldn't be unassisted,' said Henry, 'you always need someone to belay from the bottom. We could do a route up Avon Crag, it's about 50 meters with a couple of tricky stretches and we'd have to set our own anchors. It's a natural step-up from what we did this morning. What do you think?'

'What order would we climb in?' asked Tim.

'I think it best that I lead and set the anchors, Mike could follow and be guided by me. Next would be Paul and Jim, and you could belay. How does that sound?'

Paul and Jim looked at each other and decided they'd sit it out.

Mike was already packing up and five minutes later they were heading down the track to Avon Crag, a 45-minute walk across the valley.

'Thanks for sorting this,' said Mike as he and Henry walked along. 'I didn't think I'd enjoy it as much as I have.'

'No problem, it's good to do something at the weekend instead of following the missus around the shops and trying to keep tabs on the football scores,' Henry replied.

'My missus isn't like that. She realises that I need some R&R at the weekends after the pressures of the week. She pretty much lets me do as I please, providing I take her somewhere nice on Saturday night,' he grinned back.

Henry didn't say anything. Naturally, Mike not only had the perfect job, but also the perfect wife; in fact, he had the perfect life! Henry's thoughts were interrupted as they reached the start of the climb. Mike and Tim looked nervously up, but Henry, full of confidence, started readying his kit and giving instructions.

'Don't forget to double check everything,' he said, 'especially your figure of eight knot.' He'd explained earlier its importance in stopping their ropes running out of their harnesses. He glanced across as Mike did his final checks and didn't say anything.

'This isn't much different from what we did this morning. I'll lead and set an anchor every two metres. Once the first is set, Mike can start. I'll guide Mike, and Tim will remain at the bottom to control our descent. Should be straight forward and take no more than a couple of hours.' Henry looked round and saw the nods of agreement he was looking for.

Henry was enjoying the climb, guiding Mike who was coping well. It wasn't just the climb and the views, but also having Mike ask which handholds and footholds to use every couple of minutes made him feel particularly good. Half way up it started to drizzle, but they maintained a steady pace and were reassured by Tim's encouragement from the bottom.

As Henry secured the final anchor, he looked down to see Mike struggling with his harness. 'Mike, what's the problem? Whatever you do don't unclip the main buckle. I'll climb down and sort you out.' He kept his tone calm but firm.

Mike didn't say anything as Henry began slowly moving towards him.

Henry fixed another anchor to secure himself and could see that one of Mike's ropes had got caught in his harness. He moved onto a flattish bit of rock where he was next to Mike. 'Thanks, mate,' said Mike, 'I seem to have got myself in a bit of a tangle.'

Henry smiled. 'Just stand still and hold onto your ropes; I'll have to briefly unclip you to free the rope and secure your harness correctly.'

Henry's face was a picture of concentration as he started to unravel Mike's ropes. He thought he'd seen a problem with Mike's figure of eight at the bottom of the crag and wondered why he hadn't said anything. He knew what he needed to do as his fingers eased the tangled knot. His mind though was racing; all he could hear was, 'What if ...? What if ...? What if ...?' He couldn't hear the wind or feel the rain as he unclipped Mike's harness, freeing the rope. Then time stood still and his thoughts seemed to come in slow-motion. He became devoid of all awareness as he watched himself push Mike away, holding onto nothing but two unsecured ropes.

He smiled as their eyes met in the split second when Mike realised he was in freefall. He screamed as he tumbled to his death 40 metres below.

Chapter 2

The weeks after the accident had been one big blur for Henry. The paramedics had eventually arrived and announced that there was nothing they could do for Mike. They had all been questioned by the police on numerous occasions and for Henry, he could now recount his statement word for word. He relived the police interviews in his dreams.

By the time of the inquest, he had convinced himself that Mike's death had just been an unfortunate accident. Outside of the police's doubts about his role in the tragedy, friends, family and work colleagues actually saw him as a hero who had put himself at risk trying to save Mike.

He knew the police thought otherwise.

'Who was the most experienced climber?'

'Did you check Mike's equipment before he began to climb?'

'What did you see when you climbed down to Mike?'

'How is it possible that you let Mike be unsecured 40 meters up the cliff?'

Henry had been asked the same questions over and over again. He never wavered in his responses, which were backed up by the rest of the group confirming Mike was confident, verging on arrogant and that the climb had been his idea.

Paul and Jim were also under suspicion for choosing not to do that particular climb, but at the end of the day there was no evidence of any wrongdoing and no motive for the death of Mike Jones.

As Henry sat outside the Coroner's Court waiting to give evidence, his thoughts turned to the future. Like many of their friends, Carol regarded him as an unsung hero and things had definitely improved at home. Work had been difficult for everyone, but they had pulled together to keep things ticking over, with Henry insisting that he didn't need any time off.

The accident had made the local news but not the national. Henry and Tim had given a short interview to a financial reporter, Justin Kell, who wrote articles for the financial services sector. This had been limited to giving a profile of Mike's career and what he was like to work with. They'd both got on well with Kell, who'd also asked for a follow up interview once the inquest was out of the way and the dust had settled. This was part of a series he was doing on boutique fund houses and how they operate and run their funds.

As everyone expected, a 'death by accident' verdict was returned and as Henry left the court he was smiling, already planning his next move. After all he'd just got away with murder.

Despite his insistence on not taking any time off work, he'd finally agreed with John Harding that once the inquest was over, he would take a week off. This was in the hope that when he came back to work he would have cleared his head and be as ready as he could be to put the tragic episode behind him. He'd already had a couple of chats with Harding about the job he would come back to including a frank discussion of how, in view of the circumstances moving on to another firm might be best for everyone. Harding was genuinely shocked at this suggestion and was insistent that he wanted Henry to stay on and that he'd find the right role for him.

It was no surprise to Henry that on the Monday morning of his return to the office, the CEO called him in.

'Now then Henry, how was the week off?'

'Very good thanks John. Had a few days down in Brighton, lots of walking and just relaxing. I feel a lot better and raring to go.'

'OK great. Now I've been thinking about what role would be best for you and the firm. As we discussed at bonus time, I know you are keen to step up to fund manager. So, I'm going to move Tim across to run the UK Income fund and I'd like you to take over the Global Asset Growth fund from him. This will give us continuity as you settle in. We'll need to register you with the FCA, but I've had the forms drafted and they will go off today, subject to your decision.'

Henry didn't respond immediately, which created an uneasy silence in the room. He finally replied. 'Thank you, John. I'm absolutely delighted to accept.'

Harding beamed at Henry as he picked up an A4 envelope off his desk. 'Full details of the financial package are in there. I don't think you will be disappointed but come straight to me with any questions.' Harding turned to his laptop, and after a couple of clicks, turned back to face Henry. 'There! I've sent an email to all staff letting them know of your promotion. You'll be in the dealing room with Tim, so let's get you started making money for our clients.'

They stood up and shook hands across the desk. As soon as Henry stepped out into the main office, he was greeted by everyone shaking his hand, congratulatory pats on the back, wishing him well and saying how much he deserved it. It was as though Mike Jones had never existed.

Despite his confidence, Henry found the next couple of months tough, regularly referring to Tim on buy and sell decisions, fund and stock choices and interpreting the mass of data feeds from the analysts. Henry found this ironic as whilst he was an expert in preparing the Morning Star and FE data, he'd never really understood how it resulted in the decisions made by the fund managers.

Nonetheless, three months down the line he was flying solo and showing real acumen in managing the different asset classes in the fund. Back home, Carol was also getting used to the new life style. She saw Henry's pay rise as the perfect opportunity to give up her job at the hospital, replacing the toil on the wards with meeting the girls for coffee or lunch and exploring the designer shops she had not previously been able to afford.

Henry enjoyed seeing Carol happy. The mood in the house was just like when they first got married. They seldom argued and Carol accepted that his new position often required long hours and some weekend working.

It was a Friday afternoon towards the end of June when the receptionist buzzed Henry's phone saying there was a Justin Kell from the Financial Management Journal on the phone for him.

'OK,' said Henry. 'Put him through.'

'Justin, how are you?'

'Good thanks Henry. How is it going in your new role? I see that you're starting to make your mark already.'

'It's hard work, but I'm really enjoying the challenge. What can I do for you Justin?' Henry knew the reason for the call, and while he wanted to act normal and sound natural, the thought of talking to a journalist made him feel uneasy.

'Just following up on our interview a few months ago. We agreed to talk again about a series of articles I'm doing on boutique fund houses and I'm hoping you me and Tim could get together next week to do the interview.'

'Just a minute,' said Henry, putting the call on hold and turning to his colleague. 'Tim, it's that journalist Justin Kell on the phone, he wants to do an interview next week on how we run the funds. You up for that?'

'Not really, Henry. I've got the week from hell next week. You do it. It'll help raise your profile in the city.'

Despite Henry's concern at speaking to a reporter, his ego could see the plus side of doing the interview on his own. He put Justin back on the line. 'Justin, I could do the back end of next week, but Tim is busy.'

'That's ok, it's you I wanted to speak to anyway,' replied Justin. 'How about Thursday 5.30 at your office or we could do it over a drink if you like.'

Henry didn't fancy seeing Justin in the office so he replied: 'Let's do it over a drink. Do you know Boisdales on Bishopsgate? It's handy for me as it's near the station.'

'Perfect, see you then,' confirmed Justin.

Henry put the phone down and smiled to himself. *Yes*, he thought. *I can see this going very well indeed.*

Chapter 3

John Joseph Carmichael lay in his bed staring at the ceiling. He'd tossed and turned most of the night as the peace that sleep can sometimes bring evaded him. This was a day he was not looking forward to and his thoughts, both conscious and subconscious, were never far from thinking how he could avoid the humiliation it was certain to bring.

As he'd expected, his participation in Sunday's game had been limited. He was not surprised. He'd lost his focus, dedication, fitness and belief; the basic ingredients that every professional sportsman needs to have in spades if they were to make a dime out of the game. Natural ability, the skill, the art and the magic that some possessed were not his gift. He was a line-backer. Core strength, brute force and a high pain threshold were the rudimentary requirements and these had been slipping away like a thief in the night in the last few months.

He glanced at his phone, relieved to see there hadn't been any texts or calls overnight that would have been certain to add to his misery. It was still before 07.00 so he had plenty of time to pull himself together, get ready and be downtown for the 9.30 meeting that would change his life forever.

He heaved his six foot six inch frame out of bed and avoided looking at himself in the full length wardrobe door mirror as he went into the shower. Checking out the morphing of concrete quality muscle to variable ripples of unsightly fat had not been part of his morning routine since Thanksgiving, when Carrie Anne had finally kicked him out of the marital home.

In 2008 he'd been at the peak of his powers. The Reyks had the perfect season and his stats were up there in the top five. He'd secured a two-year contract extension which ended yesterday and as soon as the season ended, he'd married Carrie Anne. They'd had the twins the year before, Joseph Jnr and Hayley, and whilst it wasn't as lavish as some of the weddings of his teammates, it had not been cheap. They'd moved into a big house in the country, had a 30-foot cruiser up on the lake and lived like English royalty. For a couple of months, life had been perfect. Then one Sunday afternoon in early April, his world changed.

He'd gone up to the boat with a couple of guys to check her over after the winter. The objective was to clean things up and get everything ready for the early spring, which was generally warm and a beautiful time to be on the lake. After a couple of hours they'd finished the checks and cleaning so on the ride back to the mooring, they'd cracked open a few cans. JJ knew that his one big failing as a sportsman was that once he started drinking, he liked to keep going. After all what was the point of drinking if you didn't get the buzz! By the time they were tying up, JJ was feeling good. The beers and a couple of glasses of wine had worked their magic and he was looking forward to getting home for a late supper with Carrie Anne and hoping the twins would still be awake. The focus and concentration that are critical in top-level sport deserted him in his alcoholic buzz as he jumped onto the quay to tie up.

He slipped, lost his footing and his leg got jammed between the ten tonnes of boat and the dockside.

His knee took the brunt of the damage. Anterior cruciate ligament, medial collateral ligament and meniscus all 100% fucked. And that was the start of the journey which would finish this morning when he was to be told that his career was over and declared bankrupt.

As he stepped out of the shower, JJ wondered how things had come to this. Yes, the injury was bad but it shouldn't have been career defining. On that fateful day, the club sent a private ambulance together with one of the club doctors. Whilst everyone was happy that they could sort the knee out – eventually, the main focus of the club's hierarchy was the part booze had played. Technically, he had breached his contract. Well, actually he had breached it, being under the influence and it affecting his judgement and behaviour. This resulted in his pre-season bonus being withheld. $1m which he had already spent. Until he was back on the pitch, there would be no game time appearance cash and significantly reduced win bonuses.

The rehabilitation was slow, when he wasn't with the medics and the physios, he was at home. Carrie Anne slowly began to resent his lumbering around the house and doing the fetching and carrying that he needed and thus the downward spiral began.

As the 2009/2010 season began, it was clear he wouldn't be playing any active part. He still worked hard with the physio but as his knee improved he had more and more time on his hands to keep out from under a growingly distant Carrie Anne's feet.

Putting his jacket on and grabbing his keys from the hall table he automatically disconnected his mind from the rest of his demise. He was sure he would be reminded of it shortly.

He arranged to meet his agent, Mike Sloan, at the coffee shop they often frequented, which was just a block away from the team's corporate HQ. Mike had already got a table in the corner as the waitress delivered two Americanos.

'Hey JJ, how's it going,' Mike's standard greeting as he stood to shake JJ's hand.

'As average as usual,' replied JJ who managed a small smile. Despite everything, Mike was one of the few people who had stood by him and whilst he had been well paid at one stage, he was now supporting JJ purely pro bono. Mike had been to college and studied law, but a fondness of the extra curricula activities had cut short his time at Harvard and led him into the world of an agent for sports stars.

Blowing on his hot coffee, JJ looked across at Mike, 'What's going to happen today and how long will it take?'

Mike looked right into JJ's eyes, it was as though he was trying to see right down into his soul.

'I emailed the details through to you, but no doubt Mr Beam stopped you from reading them.' Mike didn't sound angry, but there was the usual hint of disappointment in his voice.

'The club's lawyers will start by listing the circumstances that entitles them to,' Mike counted them out on his fingers,

A. Withhold payment of bonuses that might have been earned on your contract in the last 12 months.
B. Not offer the one year option, as per the contract.
C. Withhold their share of any image rights earnings, although that is 50% of nothing

D.   Advise you that you will not be entitled to any former player privileges, which is code for don't come anywhere near the stadium, and finally.

E.   Ask you to sign an agreement not to comment adversely or negatively on any matter regarding the club, its players or officials.'

JJ just stared into his coffee as Mike went on. 'To be helpful, the club have also arranged for the IRS to attend. They will pick up at this point and go through the formalities to confirm how much you owe them and ask if you have any means to pay them back. This is where I'll come in with a list of your other debts and assets. And put forward the petition to declare you bankrupt.'

'Assets, did you say that I've got assets?'

Mike smiled and produced a few sheets of paper from his bag. Waiving them in front of JJ he said. 'This my friend is your get out of jail free card.'

When they entered a modest sized meeting room on the 12th floor of the Reyks HQ, there were two faces they recognised and one they didn't. The greetings were formal and polite but there was no small talk. The guy they didn't know was introduced to them as Ed Zealand, the team's senior lawyer and Board member.

'Following a meeting of the Board yesterday evening, 28th February 2010, it was determined by a unanimous vote that'… JJ switched off as Zealand read through the same points that Mike had advised him of earlier. Zealand finished with 'any questions' and clearly expecting there not to be any as he started gathering his papers.

Raising his hand almost like a kid in school, Mike interjected. 'Just a couple of quick questions Ed. Firstly, as JJ has no contract and no income, would the club consider paying a modest severance payment to help him get back on his feet. And secondly, when JJ signed his contract two years ago the club took out a life assurance policy on him for $10m which only pays out on death. As the club no longer has an interest in this policy, could this be signed over to JJ who would then maintain the annual premiums?'

Ed Zealand steepled his fingers, leaning forward to rest his chin on them. He didn't look at his two colleagues as he considered the requests. 'As to the question of any severance payment, the answer is no. There are no clauses relating to any payments once the contract is concluded or terminated for a valid reason.' His tone and demeanour were emotionless. He went on, 'as to the life assurance contract, I agree that the club no longer has an insurable interest in JJ, so yes, we would be happy to assign this over to JJ. I would, however, point out that the annual premium for 2010 is due next month on 1st April. I will arrange for the necessary papers to be couriered over to you later today.' With that he stood up and left the room. The meeting was over.

Tony Chalker, the club's media liaison guy and Phil Budman, the contracts manager remained and went straight into full schmooze mode. They were sorry it had come to this, they were here to help JJ if they could, let's keep in touch. After the pleasantries it was time for the second feature. The meeting with the IRS and the Insolvency Service.

Chalker and Budman left the room and a few minutes later two replicas of Ed Zealand appeared. They introduced themselves but JJ's mind was a blur. Mr IRS started by stating that JJ owed $648,321 in unpaid taxes and that interest would start to accrue if the full amount was not paid in 30 days.

It was then Mr Insolvency's turn to speak, just like a double act that had been performing together for years. 'We've reviewed the list of Mr Carmichael's assets and liabilities provided by Mr Sloan and verified that they reflect Mr Carmichael's circumstances. We understand that the two properties are in joint ownership with Mrs Carmichael and are in the process of being sold. There is a boat that is owned solely by Mr Carmichael and again this is being sold.'

'Cut to the chase,' said Mike. 'We know all this. What is the 'net' position you guys would be happy with.'

'After mortgages and loans have been repaid, and Mrs Carmichael has received her share of the proceeds. Mr Carmichael, has just over $100,000 to his name.' Mr Insolvency put his pen down that he'd been using to trace his way down the page he was reading from, indicating he'd finished for now.

The meeting went on for another two hours and if Mike was being paid he would have certainly earned his money.

The deal they carved out was straightforward and provided JJ with a chance of redemption. He was declared bankrupt. The

IRS agreed to settle for 10 cents on the dollar, which left JJ with just about $30,000 to help him get back on his feet. It was unlikely he would see much of this as Carrie Anne had already started divorce proceedings and whilst he couldn't contest anything she wanted, as it had already been taken away from him, he didn't expect $30,000 to go very far.

The meeting concluded with the signing of the required papers and Mike and JJ headed back to the coffee shop to take stock.

'That went well then,' smiled Mike as he blew on his coffee. 'Nice straight edge, so we can start getting you sorted.'

'After Carrie Anne's finished with me, I won't have enough money to buy a loaf of bread, yet alone pay next month's rent!' JJ replied.

Mike continued, ignoring his friend's rant, 'First, a couple of ground rules. Consider these a pre-requisite for my ongoing love and support. You give the booze up completely. If you have to, go to an AA meeting, but you have to get yourself clean. Then you get a job. Any job to start with, just to get you out of the house each day and into a routine. You manage this for six months and then we re-plan. By this time I should be able to inject considerable funds in project JJ Carmichael.'

For the first time since his downward spiral, JJ looked at his friend and felt truly ashamed. He thought of the people he'd let down in the last two years. His teammates, his wife, his kids, his friends, the fans and most of all himself. He was crying as he managed to whisper. 'Sure, anything you say Mike. I mean it, I really mean it.'

When JJ had composed himself, he leaned across the table and hugged Mike until he gasped, 'thanks JJ but I'm struggling to breathe.' They both laughed and JJ said, 'OK what's the play?

'Remember when Zealand agreed to sign over the life policy to you,' JJ nodded and Mike continued, 'Well, I'm going to sell it and make us rich.'

Chapter 4

Justin Kell finished the call with Henry Gray and added the details to his diary. When he'd met with Henry and Tim Fleming a few months earlier, he'd been struck that Gray spoke like he'd memorised his responses and was going to stick to the script come what may, even if he didn't really answer the question.

Maybe it was the policeman in Justin that made him sceptical about the accident that had befallen Mike Jones. In his ten years at the Met, he'd come across hundreds of liars and could generally suss out within a few minutes whether they were telling the truth or not. He hadn't got a strong sense that Gray was lying through his teeth but he was confident that he wasn't telling the whole truth.

Mike Jones had been a bit of a rising star in the fund management community, gaining a reputation for delivering solid fund performance despite the prevailing economic conditions of the time. The CAM funds hadn't suffered as much as most during the recent crash and he'd picked up that some of the larger houses were looking at recruiting him. Now he was dead and the guy who was right there at that fateful moment had taken over his job. It was too much of a coincidence and he didn't believe in coincidences.

In the lead up to the meeting with Kell, Henry Gray went through the same preparation as he had following Mike's death. He wrote down all the questions he thought he could be asked about the time following Mike's death, the police enquiry, the questions he was asked, the Coroner's Court and how he'd ended up with his promotion. He knew that this was overkill as the interview would focus on CAM, its culture and the challenges of being a small firm in a very big pond. But he didn't want anything he said to raise suspicion in the mind of a journalist, who was famous for his investigative work following various financial scandals that had hit the city in recent years.

By the time Thursday came, Gray was confident the meeting would go well and hopefully the exposure he would get would help in building his reputation as a decent fund manager. He'd discussed what he was going to say with Tim and John Harding and they were comfortable he was on message as far as the firm was concerned.

He left the office just before 5.30 pm. It would take him about ten minutes to walk up to Boisdales and thought there was no harm in keeping Kell waiting.

As expected, he saw Kell sitting at the far end of the bar with a vacant stool beside him, which he'd hung his jacket on. It reminded Henry of various holidays he'd had with Carol, when he got up at 6.30 just to secure the best sun beds with their towels.

The spot at the end of the bar was ideal for a private discussion. The noise level from the Thursday crowd was sufficient to avoid being overheard and the remaining stools were down at the other end of the bar.

'Henry, good to see you again. What would you like to drink?' Kell said as he held out his hand in greeting.

'Pint of Asahi, please Justin,' replied Henry, warmly shaking Kell's hand.

They exchanged the usual pleasantries about the weather, what the FTSE had done that day and the likelihood of a general election next year, before Kell moved on to what they were there to talk about.

'Let's start with some facts about you please, Henry. If you could give me a quick rundown of your career to date, the companies you've been with, positions you've held and professional qualifications and I'll do my best to include them in the article to give your profile a bit of coverage.' Henry looked at Kell, but before he could say anything Kell went on. 'I found during my time at the Met that getting people to talk about themselves usually helps the discussion flow a lot better.'

'You were at the Met?' Henry spluttered, before quickly regaining his composure. 'That's interesting, when did you move into journalism?'

'My degree was in journalism, but I'd always wanted to be a cop since I was kid. When I graduated I applied for the graduate scheme, which was designed to fast track you through the ranks. I loved it at first, but over the years the increasing red tape made the job more difficult and less enjoyable. Then something happened and I decided to leave. Anyway, we're not here to talk about me, please tell me about how you got into the industry.'

Gray took a large pull on his second pint of Asahi and sketched out the outline of his career to date. Once he got started, he relaxed a little. Maybe it was the lager kicking in or just that he felt on safe ground as he kept well away from any mention of Mike Jones.

'And then I started at CAM in 2007 as a junior analyst.' Gray thought that was a good point to stop. He didn't want to get into more recent events so he tried to steer the conversation to back to how CAM operated, its culture and strategy.

'So what do you want to know about CAM itself?' Gray asked, noting that Kell was still only halfway down his first pint, while he had just started his third.

'An insight in what it's like to work there; I'm not looking for any trade secrets, but CAM is a growing and successful business, so the philosophy of its approach to managing clients' money and the relationship you have with them,' Kell smiled, noticing that Henry almost breathed a sigh of relief as he rushed into the standard corporate patter he'd no doubt memorised during the last few days.

Twenty minutes later, Henry had no more to say. He'd exhausted the topics he and John Harding had agreed he should cover and realised he'd repeated himself on more than one occasion.

Kell said, 'thanks Henry that's great. I've enough for the feature when I add in the bits and pieces that are in the public domain. Are you happy that I position it as an interview with you with quotes where appropriate? I'll send you a draft before publication.'

'Sure,' replied Henry. 'If you've got what you need, I'll be off as my train is in ten minutes.' He slipped of his stool and was putting his jacket on when Kell came back with.

'Just one more, thing.' Kell paused for a moment looking at Henry. 'Mike Jones, it was a terrible accident.'

'Yes it was,' replied Henry.

'How do you feel about stepping into his shoes? You must have mixed feelings about benefiting from his untimely death?'

'No comment,' muttered Henry. He pushed his way through the crowded bar, bumping into people and spilling drinks as he went. Kell watched him go, thinking, *thanks Henry, I don't think you'd be a very good poker player*.

Henry got a seat on the 19.58 from Liverpool Street back to Braintree. He was fuming as much with himself as that toad Kell. How could he have been so stupid! Letting him buy him all those drinks, lulling him into a false sense of security and then hitting him with the 'Mike Jones' sucker punch at the end. He would have to think about what he was going to do about Justin bloody Kell. Yes, he would have to think very carefully.

The next morning Justin Kell was back in his office, going over his notes from his meeting with Henry Gray. The article itself would be straight forward, fitting nicely into the series he was doing on boutique fund houses. The matter of Gray's involvement in Mike Jones' death was anything but straightforward. Certainly getting any proof would be difficult. He decided he'd make a couple of calls to his contacts at the Met and see if they could give him the details of the investigating officer over in Avon and Somerset. That would be his first step in discovering the truth about Mike Jones' untimely death.

Chapter 5

At 37, Justin Kell had progressed well in his second career as a journalist. His inquiring mind and easy way with people from all walks of life, added to a natural journalistic talent had seen his reputation grow in the financial press. When he left the Met in 2004, it was an obvious choice to use his degree and go into journalism. As a good all round sportsman, he continued to play football most weeks and the occasional game of golf in the summer, so initially he looked into being a freelance sports writer. Despite his natural interest in all things sport, he found writing about it far less interesting than playing or watching. So when a position came up at the FMJ, he applied and to his surprise, got the job.

Despite the manner of his leaving his Inspector's job, he still had a number of contacts there who were always happy to meet him for a drink after their shift and catch up on what was new as well as reminiscing on the good old days.

He rang the main switchboard and asked to be put through to Chris Packham, who he regarded as a friend as well as an ex-colleague.

'Chris, its Justin, how's it going?'

'Well if it isn't ace reporter Justin Kell, who must want something if he's ringing just a lowly Detective Inspector like me.' Packham's tone was genial and they settled into a quick exchange of how they were, how their respective jobs were going and general small talk, before Packham said: 'What is it you want Justin?'

'I don't know if you remember a few months back, a London fund manager called Mike Jones, fell to his death in a rock climbing accident down in Bristol. The Coroner came back with a verdict of accidental death, but I'm starting to have some reservations.'

Kell went through everything he had on Henry Gray, including his reaction to the mention of Mike Jones at the end of their meeting yesterday evening. Like a good copper, Chris Packham just listened and Justin could almost hear him jotting down the key points of his story. When he had finished, Packham said.

'I do recall the incident. As you know, if there is anything unusual or suspicious about a death of someone on our patch, we get the details as a matter of course. But we weren't asked to give any assistance and when it was confirmed as death by accident, we closed the file. What would you like me to do Justin?'

'I was hoping you could contact the lead investigation officer down in Bristol. See what they thought of Henry Gray. Are there any loose ends that they aren't comfortable with and if possible get copies of the statements from the other guys involved as well as Gray'

Packham laughed. 'You don't want much, do you Justin. This will cost you a curry and a few pints when I next get some time off. Leave it with me and I'll call you when I have something.'

'Thanks Chris and I'll let you know if anything develops at my end. I'm writing an article on Gray's firm based on the meeting we had. I can't be explicit with my concerns, but I'm going to try to get a reaction from him.' With that, they ended the call and Kell began to sketch out the article on Chartered Asset Management and Henry Gray.

At the same time Justin Kell was sharing his concerns over Henry Gray regarding the death of Mike Jones; the man himself was sitting in his office pondering on how he should deal with the scum of a reporter.

Gray had convinced himself that he could not let anything to do with Mike Jones' death reappear in the public domain. He thought about ringing Kell to apologise for how he left the bar, saying that the emotion of Mike's death was still raw and mixed with one beer too many, pushed him to his atypical reaction. He could ask to meet him again, on the promise to give more insight for his article. Or he could go on the offensive and demand that the article does not get published.

But Gray knew that all these potential courses of action would be pointless. Justin Kell was an ex copper turned reporter.

He wouldn't give up on a potential scoop just because he apologised and tried to smooth things over. No, he would need to find another way, beginning with what he could find out about Justin Kell, particularly why he had left the Met. Maybe, if there was some skeleton in Kell's cupboard, he could exploit it. If not, he might have to consider a more drastic course of action. Kell had said he would send a draft of the article through, before it went to print, so Gray guessed he had a couple of weeks to find out what he could about who he was starting to regard as the enemy.

It only took Kell a couple of days to draft the article on CAM, putting Henry front and centre. What he was finding more difficult, was how to include anything on the Mike Jones affair that would get people thinking about Gray's involvement without writing anything libellous. He had a number of other stories he was working on, so he decided to park the series on boutique fund houses until he heard back from Chris Packham. After all, it wouldn't do any harm to let Gray sweat for a while. And Kell was certain that he was sweating.

Chapter 6

For the first few weeks after his insolvency meeting, JJ heeded Mike's words and in his mind made significant strides in cleaning up his act. He was only having a couple of drinks at weekends, after all Mike had said he should get into a routine. He'd found himself a job at a local High School, in the sports department, basically as the janitor. He would open up the sports halls and changing rooms first thing. Make sure the kit and equipment was clean and fit for purpose and then tidy up at the end of each session, put the gear and equipment away and then clean the changing rooms and the showers.

Of course, everyone knew who he was and he got asked for the odd selfie, but the principal, who was a big fan, had positioned it that JJ wanted "to give something back", and set an example that simple hard work was a virtuous pursuit.

JJ liked the work and loved the routine. After his first week, he was asked to help out with football practice, which he found more enjoyable than actually playing. When word got out that he was doing this, the after school sessions grew quite a crowd to watch him help put the kids through their paces.

Come Friday afternoons, he got what city workers would call, 'the Friday afternoon feeling'. Which was code for heading to your favourite bar and drinking away the stresses of the week. JJ didn't have any stresses he wanted to get rid of, but he did want to renew his acquaintance with Jim Beam.

He knew that Mike would not view this part of his new "routine" favourably, but just a couple of hits at Declans, which was conveniently just around the corner from his apartment and maybe a couple more throughout the evening was enough to keep his demons away. He'd made up a rule that he wouldn't drink if he was working the next day which provided more self-justification to enjoy Friday and Saturday nights. It was also why he had politely declined to get involved in the weekend fixtures for the school football team.

When Mike finally got in touch, he met JJ after he'd finished at the school one Thursday afternoon. They found a local coffee shop and a table in the corner where no one would disturb them.

'You look like you've lost weight.' Mike's opening statement took JJ a little by surprise.

'Maybe a little,' he responded. 'I don't need to monitor it like I used to. I don't think the kids at school are bothered by my BMI.'

'You eating properly?' came back Mike.

'Christ Mike, you're not my mother!'

'I know, I know. It's just that we need you to be in a certain state of health for a medical I'm lining up for you.'

'What medical? I don't need any medical. What are you on about Mike?'

'Remember we got that life policy out of the insolvency meeting. Well I've been making enquiries about selling it.'

'Selling it! Who would want to buy a shitty life policy on my life?' JJ said incredulously.

'There are these firms who put all kinds of assets into their funds. It's not just cash and stocks and shares these days. Vintage cars, fine wines, gold, precious metals and the latest fad is life policies.'

JJ laughed. 'How does that work then?'

'It's very simple. Your policy will pay out $100m when you die. The "fund", will buy it off you for about 10 cents on the dollar. You get $1m and they benefit from the settlement when you pass. You benefit from the cash now and they get an asset for their fund. Simple.'

It sounded far from simple to JJ and he just looked at his friend waiting for greater enlightenment.

Mike went over the concept a couple more times before JJ thought he understood. 'So, I sign over the policy to some investment house. They give me a load of dollars, and then in 50 years' time when I'm ready to meet the good Lord, they get the full $100m.'

'Exactly,' said Mike. 'There are just a couple of things we need to sort out. Firstly, the main market for these fund managers are the elderly. People who haven't got long to live, have a policy but need some cash now for medical fees or nursing home rent or simply to blow on hookers in Vegas. And secondly, you JJ are 32 and despite your addictions, will probably live to a ripe old age. Also, very few firms look to hold individual assets for 30 odd years, but there are one or two setting up that are taking a longer term view.'

'And that's where this medical comes in.' The light had pinged on for JJ.

'Exactly,' said Mike. 'Which is why we need to consider your 'addictions.'

JJ tried not to look uncomfortable. 'I'm doing OK you know Mike. Getting myself clean. I've got a job and a responsibility to the school and kids.'

'But I know you JJ. I know about the Friday afternoons in Declans and the trips to the liquor store on Saturdays. How much are you getting through?'

'Enough to keep me functioning,' replied JJ. 'But I'm off the pain killers, no drugs at all.'

There was a long silence as they sipped their coffee and got refills from the waitress.

Mike didn't look up when he said quietly. 'What I'm about to say, I'm saying cos I'm your friend. So trust me and we can both start to get our lives back on track, with some proper money behind us.' JJ thought his life was getting back on track but let Mike carry on.

'How much do you think you could control the drinking? If you went back to the two bottles a day phase? What I mean is, if you slipped back into that life style, could you come back out of it again, like you've just done?'

JJ missed the point his friend was trying to make. 'I'm not going to slip back Mike. I've got my job and starting to enjoy life. OK, I still have a drink at the weekends but I'm not going back to those bad old days.'

Mike's discomfort was visible as he went on. He knew he had to be blunt. 'What I'm actually saying is that in order to get the maximum value for your policy, we need you to be in the poorest health of your life. It would only need to be for say six months. You'd have a medical which helps them work out your life expectancy, and the shorter that is, the more money they pay

33

you. I'm only suggesting this as your friend and knowing that you could pull yourself around again just as you are doing now.'

JJ finally understood the phrase, 'jaw dropping.' He stared open mouthed at Mike before picking up his drink and throwing it in his now ex-friend's face. He did not say a word as he stood up and left, leaving Mike dripping in lukewarm coffee.

Chapter 7

Henry Gray might be a decent fund manager, but he quickly realised he was a poor sleuth. He tried to find out as much as he could about Justin Kell, but with not having any police contacts, he was limited to what he could find out online.

He'd gone to a grammar school in the north of England, got a first class degree in journalism from Manchester University and joined the Met in 1994. As with most police profiles, there was little detail on his career other than the promotions and when he left in 2004, there was little detail on the reasons. The best he could find was a quote from the Chief Inspector, that 'after a distinguished period of service, Inspector Kell left for health related and personal reasons.' Gray did not have any connections in the police, so he had no idea what he could do next to find out more about the reporter.

At the same time that Gray had reached his dead end, the phone rang on Justin Kell's desk. He answered with his usual 'Kell' and heard the familiar voice of Chris Packham on the other end of the line. 'Hi Justin, I've been making those enquiries you asked about and I might have something for you. It's not much, but probably worth a curry and a couple of pints.'

'OK sounds interesting, when can you get away?' replied Kell.

'Thursday's good for me,' said Packham. 'How about HDQ at 6.00 and then we can go round the corner for a curry.'

'Great, see you then,' said Kell, smiling to himself as he put the phone down.

The Hung Drawn and Quartered was as busy as usual and Kell and Packham just chatted about the old times. It was only when they had ordered their curries in the Rajasthan at the bottom of Monument Street that Packham said.

'I spoke to Avon and Somerset, the Inspector who led the investigation was very helpful, mainly because he too has doubts about Henry Gray's involvement.' Kell knew not to interrupt his friend's flow so said nothing and listened intently.

Packham continued. 'In a case like this, it's always going to be very unlikely that there will be any physical evidence. Fingerprints are meaningless and nobody saw anything, until Mike Jones went hurtling past them down the cliff. But there are inconsistencies in the statements of events immediately prior to the climb. Avon and Somerset are satisfied that the two guys who didn't climb are telling the truth. Their stories are consistent. They aren't the best of climbers and they didn't like Mike Jones' gung-ho approach to what they saw as a difficult climb. But here's the interesting thing, in their statements they both said that Gray always checked everyone's equipment, ropes, knots etc. before every climb and they are "reasonably" certain that Gray only had a cursory look at Jones' before the fatal climb. Gray however, maintains that he did do the full check despite Jones confirming he had double checked everything and was keen to start the climb.

'If Gray's version of the events are to be believed, this supports his assertion that when Jones got into difficulty, he panicked and started fiddling with his equipment and detaching his harness from the ropes.

'Also, in a situation like this it's not unusual, for the most experienced climber, Gray, to go first on a climb. But when Jones got into trouble, the standard procedure would be to bring them both down. "On belay" they call it. Gray claims that he climbed down to Jones because he saw he was panicking and he thought he could calm him down and get him climbing again. When he got to Jones, Gray claims that Jones was fumbling with his harness and the figure of eight knot which is critical. But this wouldn't be the case if everything had been checked as OK at the start of the climb. The view is that no one can understand how Jones could not be attached to the ropes and anchor points which made his fall possible. There is a view that Gray had some involvement, not necessarily intentionally, but he has stuck to his story throughout.'

Packham stopped for a mouth full of biryani, so Kell interjected.

'So the conclusion was Gray had some involvement, but nothing can be proved. And now he's benefitting from Jones's death, hoping it will all be forgotten'

'Got it in one,' said Packham. 'None of the team down in Bristol liked or believed Gray. They thought he was shifty and just kept repeating the same story word for word.'

'This could explain why he reacted the way he did when I mentioned Jones' death to him the other week,' said Kell. 'But unless he decides to confess there's no way the truth of actually what happened that day will come out.'

They finished their meals and Kell picked up the tab as promised. 'Thanks Chris, it's not much but I think I can rattle Gray's cage a bit with what you've given me.'

They said their goodbyes and despite the hour Kell headed back to the office to put the finishing touches to the article on Chartered Asset Management and Henry Gray. If he finished tonight, he could send the draft to Gray tomorrow as he'd promised and wait and see what reaction he got.

Before he sent the draft, Kell had one more call to make. He had spoken to Mike Jones' wife, Fiona, last month about the article in general and promised to show it to her before publication. She'd been holding up well since the death of her husband and had left a message on Kell's phone to give her a call. She answered in a surprisingly bright voice and sounded happy to hear from him so quickly.

'Thanks for the article Justin, I'm not bothered about what Gray has to say, he's a real shit. But I really appreciate the footnote about Mike's contribution and thanks again for your best wishes.'

The investigator in Kell couldn't help asking, 'why are you calling Gray a real shit?'

'Mike thought he was a creep. He always appeared dissatisfied with his lot and was very jealous of Mike and Tim, particularly their jobs and the life style that went with it. He was always making suggestions to Mike about how to interpret the data he provided, implying he could do things better. Mike just didn't like him. Anyway, enough of my ramblings, thanks for sending the article and particularly how you mention Mike. Goodbye Justin.'

As he put down the phone, Justin thought, *another piece of circumstantial evidence.*

The next day at 16.38, an email from Justin Kell appeared in Henry Gray's inbox. His heart sank as he considered whether to open the attachment immediately or leave it until Monday morning. It didn't take him long to decide, as he knew that either way, he'd be worrying about it over the weekend.

As he read the article, he relaxed a little as the content was a decent summary of CAM as a business, very positive about how the operation was run and also painted a picture of Henry Gray as a capable, safe pair of hands. It wasn't until the footnote at the end, that Gray couldn't believe what he was reading.

Henry Gray refused to make any comment about Mike Jones' influence to the success of CAM Ltd or the tragic circumstances of the accident that led to his death. Gray, an experienced climber was with Jones on the cliff when he fell. FMJ would like to acknowledge the contribution that Mike made in the world of fund management and send our ongoing best wishes to his family.

Gray picked the phone and dialled Kell's direct line. When he answered on the second ring Gray fumed, 'You can't print this, its libellous! It makes me sound like I don't give a shit about Mike.'

Kell responded in a calm understated voice, 'Two things Henry. It's not libellous, it's an accurate record of our interview and I have a recording on my phone. Also, you don't give a shit about Mike Jones and I'm going to prove it. Have a nice day Henry.' And with that he put the phone down.

Chapter 8

The article didn't get much of a reaction in the fund management community. The CEO of CAM, John Harding, got a few calls which were all positive. Gray had explained to him that he was still upset over Mike's death which was why he didn't want to talk about it, and that he was fuming about how it had been reflected in the article.

Harding wasn't concerned about how Henry Gray came out of it, so long as CAM got the right publicity. He was happy Gray was doing a decent job but he didn't really like him, so if he took some flak for a while, so be it.

One person who was very interested in how Henry Gray came across in the article was Alfio Mignemi. Having read it three times over breakfast in the apartment at Devonshire Place, he spent the rest of the morning researching everything on the death of Mike Jones. When he was satisfied he had everything he needed, he picked up the burner mobile he was currently using and dialled one of the two numbers stored in it.

His call was picked up straight away, but as per the usual protocol, only he spoke. 'I've found the person we are looking for. His name is Henry Gray and he works at Chartered Asset Management in the city. He is capable and has the personality traits that are required. I will make contact this week and advise progress accordingly.' He ended the call.

Mignemi always enjoyed working in London. His associates permanently rented the Devonshire Place apartment which was ideally located for getting about the city. There are some outstanding restaurants nearby and people like himself could generally go unnoticed. He'd had his current identity validated eighteen months ago, when he had fronted a significant investment on behalf of his associates into a hedge fund that had inside information on a failing securities house. The fund and the authorities had accepted him and the source of funds as legitimate and the rest had been straight forward.

He liked the persona of Alfio Mignemi, a 52-year-old Italian "entrepreneur", and he looked the part. Six feet tall with slicked back black hair and a touch of grey at the temples. He was fluent in a number of languages but was always more comfortable when speaking in his native Italian.

As he left the apartment, he called the other number in his phone. 'Robert, I've found the man we are looking for. I'm on my way to meet him now. If all goes well, I'll arrange for the three of us to meet in the next couple of days.'

Mignemi had called ahead to Gray's office, posing as a high roller who was interested in investing in the CAM funds. He'd insisted on meeting with Gray alone as he respected him as a fund manager and only wanted one point of contact with the firm. They'd fallen over themselves to free up Gray's diary to meet him, and his appointment was made for 11.30.

Mignemi enjoyed the short stroll down Bishopsgate in the early summer sunshine and when he arrived at CAM's office he was immediately shown into the standard meeting room where there was coffee and the choice of still and sparkling water. An espresso and bottle of sparkling were dutifully put in front of him by the receptionist and seconds later, Gray walked in and they exchanged introductions.

'I understand you are considering investing in our funds?' Gray thought it best to get straight to the point.

'No Mr Gray, my associates are looking to invest in you, and make you a very wealthy man.'

'Sorry, I don't understand,' replied a bemused Gray.

'You are a very good fund manager Mr Gray. My associates are looking for someone with your talents to manage a new fund that we intend to launch this summer. I am offering you the job with a basic salary of double what you are currently earning, plus the potential for significant bonuses, subject to your performance.'

Gray was stunned not knowing what to say next. So Mignemi filled the silence.

'I would like you to meet the CEO of the company tomorrow evening over dinner. We will discuss in detail the nature of the fund, the business model and your role. We need to move quickly and will expect your acceptance tomorrow. Subject to this you will resign your position here immediately and if necessary, we will buy you out of any restrictive covenants. We are serious Henry, trust me we are very serious.'

Gray was in a daze as he went back to his office after the meeting. *Had he just been offered a job? Why was his mysterious visitor so insistent that he was the man they were looking for and most importantly, what could he do with all that money.* He didn't see any harm in going for a nice dinner to find out more, after all he could always say no.

The dinner meeting was at the Duck and Waffle on Bishopsgate; 7.00 pm and don't be late Mignemi had said. So Gray dutifully arrived at five to seven and saw Mignemi standing at the bar with another guy, similar in height and build to Mignemi but probably ten years younger.

'Henry, thank you for being on time.' Mignemi shook Henry's hand and turned to the man on his left. This is Robert Dulac, the CEO of the Horizon Settlement Fund.

'Pleased to meet you Henry, oh and everyone calls me Bobby,' said Dulac with a strong New York accent.

'I've booked a private room for us,' said Mignemi nodding to the head waiter who was clearly waiting for the signal. He took his cue, 'This way please gentlemen.'

The room was very spacious and they were shown to the only table which was at the far end. Once they were seated and the waiter had left, Mignemi said. 'We will complete our business before we order, this will give us plenty of time for your questions over dinner. Robert, over to you.'

Dulac was more relaxed with a conversational tone.

'It's probably best if you let me go through everything before you ask your questions Henry. It's a simple business model but I will go into as much detail as you need.'

Gray nodded and Dulac continued.

'You may be aware that in the States there are a small number of funds being launched, that describe themselves as Life Settlement Funds. The concept is simple. The funds buy up life policies from people who need to raise some cash. The target market is the over 50s, who usually have some health issues. Subject to a medical and a mortality calculation the fund buys the policy for a percentage on the dollar. In the States, the obesity rates of adults is 35% and rising. This increases as people get older. The healthcare situation is patchy throughout America, nothing like your NHS. This results in reduced impaired life expectancy with the result that any life policy which falls into our parameters can produce an attractive return.'

Dulac paused for a sip of his water before continuing.

'It's not unusual for people to fall behind with their premiums, after all why pay the $50 monthly premium when that equates to a weekend feast at Macky Dees. We have sources in the main life offices who are happy to provide us with the details of these individuals; not entirely legal, but hey, everyone is happy. And we use these to target our mailings. We also advertise the service in local papers, which produces positive results, and once someone is interested, it only takes a couple of weeks to sign the policy over to us.'

Gray was engrossed in Dulac's pitch and he wasn't running out of steam.

'A typical example would be that a client has a life policy that pays out $250k when they croak. They are a few months behind with the premiums when we contact them. We pay them anything from ten to twenty five grand subject to the medical; we start paying the premiums including any arrears and that's that. The dude dies within two years and the fund nets the $250k. Occasionally we will acquire a high value policy on a younger life to support our net asset ratio, but in short that's the model.'

It appeared that Dulac had finished until Mignemi prompted him with, 'and the regulatory position.'

'Of course, the fund is well capitalised by Mr Mignemi and his associates and will be based in Dublin and managed here in London by you. The application papers just need your details as the Approved Person who will manage the fund, which after this evening we expect to submit to the FCA tomorrow.'

Mignemi picked up the flow.

'We will pay a basic salary of £250k a year, plus benefits, plus bonuses. If you join us by the first of August, you will receive a golden hello of £100k. We will make arrangements for you to receive this tax free; Robert will go through the details in due course. Now, I suggest we order and discuss your questions and some of the practical arrangements while we eat.'

Gray relaxed as the meal went on with Mignemi and Dulac answering all his questions. As they ordered coffee, Gray asked, 'So why me? This is an unbelievable opportunity and there are loads of fund managers in the city with more experience than me.'

It was Mignemi who replied. 'You have all the qualities that we are looking for, in the broadest sense. We are a small team and everyone needs to get involved in all aspects of the business and we believe that you have the attributes that we require. Now, let's talk about your resignation that you will be handing in tomorrow.'

It irked Gray that they hadn't actually formally asked him if he wanted the job. They had assumed from the moment he walked into the restaurant that he had said yes. He realised these were not the type of people you said no to, and after all there was a £100k tax free signing on bonus! He couldn't wait to get home and tell Carol.

Chapter 9

Amy Speight sat at her desk in her Manchester office staring intently at her laptop. To anyone watching her for the last three hours it would appear that she was expecting the numbers on the screen to change at her will. They didn't of course.

She glanced at the clock on the wall and was not surprised to see that it was nearly midnight. Phone calls to her American suppliers had been fruitless. No one was prepared to extend her exhausted lines of credit or supply any further stock until her account was brought up to date. The only minor success of the evening was that she'd managed to persuade her handling agent in London to suspend his legal action for the unpaid commission he was owed.

Shutting her laptop down, she rubbed her eyes, stood up and stretched her arms above her head. She realised time was short and tomorrow's meeting with the banking syndicate could not be postponed any longer.

Leaning back in her chair, she closed her eyes and thought back to the days it had all started.

Life was so simple when she left university in 2001. She'd graduated from Manchester with a first class business and marketing degree and got the first job she'd applied for at an advertising agency in Spinningfields, selling space to 'upper market' magazines like Cheshire Life and Horse and Hounds. Eighteen months in, two things happened; first she was bored. The routine was killing her and there was zero creative flair required to hit her targets. Second, she met Peter. They met in Pret just outside her office. As usual, she was the only one prepared to do the morning coffee run and there in front of her in the queue was this drop dead gorgeous guy, who smiled at her like she was the only person in the world. From then on, Amy made sure she did the coffee run every day and sure enough,

Peter was there either in the queue or sitting at a table reading the FT sipping his flat white.

The courtship dance developed when he asked her to join him for coffee one day and the rest as they say is history. He worked for Deloitte in Corporate Finance, was a couple of years older than her and didn't have any emotional hang-ups. The boredom at work magically disappeared as their relationship blossomed. All her attention and energy was focussed on Peter and having fun. They moved into a small two bedroom flat in the city centre and once they settled into the routine of being a "proper couple", the realisation of how much her job sucked moved up the league table of her priorities of things she needed to sort out.

It was Peter who suggested the idea of setting up her own agency. The start-up costs would be small. She could use the second bedroom that was already set up as an office for Peter when he worked from home and take it from there.

So on 3rd March 2004, AmDesigns Ltd was born.

Back then she'd enjoyed the fourteen hour days as she grew the business. Her market was a broad canvas. She'd picked up promotional work from a diverse range of businesses and sectors. Fashion brands, retail shops, hotels and even an engineering company. Her pitch was personal service, twenty four hours a day, seven days a week.

As the business grew, she moved out of the back bedroom, started to employ staff, diversified into beauty products and treatments and built a brand of her own. The big break came in early 2006 when the Elite Hotel Group approached her to take on the beauty salons and spa facilities in their 15 strong chain of UK hotels. They provided the finance at a knock down rate and let her maintain her own branding. Elite simply wanted a first class experience for their clients and were happy with market rate rent on the space Amy rented in their hotels.

She managed a smile as she switched the lights off in the office and caught the lift to the ground floor. Her mind was able to remember the happy, fun times, but seemed to shut off when the financial crash of 2008 hit, which was the start of the downward spiral. AmDesigns was likely to receive its coup de grace tomorrow.

She called a taxi and headed home to Didsbury where Peter would be asleep in the spare bedroom. They had moved there last year and she loved being able to get out of the city and to have a house with a decent sized garden.

'Any joy yesterday?' asked Peter over breakfast.

'Not really,' replied Amy. 'I managed to persuade Carlos in London that I'd get things sorted soon and he'd get his commission, but the banks aren't budging and neither are the suppliers. Everyone wants cash that I just haven't got. I'm holding a mountain of stock, that I can't sell, three of my biggest clients have gone bust, owing me thousands and the banks are treating me like an infectious disease.'

'It was a good job we put the house in your name,' she went on, 'otherwise we could be looking for somewhere else to live by the end of the week.'

Peter nervously pushed his porridge around the bowl, lowered his eyes and speaking very quietly said, 'This is probably the worst time this could come up but I've been offered a promotion and it's in Sydney. I've known for the last couple of weeks but didn't want to tell you with all you had on, but I need to let them know one way or another today.'

The frozen look on Amy's face portrayed the shock, disappointment, betrayal and treachery she felt at Peter's impending abandonment of her. 'And of course you are going to say yes.' Her voice was calm despite the tumult of emotion she felt.

'Yes, I leave at the weekend. Once you've got yourself sorted out you can come and join me.'

'Come and join you! Fuck off Peter I never want to see you again.'

With that, Peter left for work and true to her word, Amy did not see him ever again.

The meeting with the banks was at the HSBC UK HQ in Canary Wharf that evening. Amy had already packed her overnight bag and she was booked on the 11.33 out of Piccadilly which would get into Euston just over a couple of hours later. She'd arranged to meet her accountant at 2.30 to go over the latest figures and plan their strategy to try and get a stay of execution, otherwise they planned to put AmDesigns Group Ltd into voluntary administration.

Despite Amy knowing the numbers from the various divisions of the Group almost by heart, Phil Jones, her accountant insisted on going over them all as they met in a meeting room of a serviced office in Canary Wharf of one of his other clients.

'The only division that is potentially viable at this stage is the salons in the Elite hotels. I can't see any way to save the product manufacturing company and the distribution division only works when there is a consistent flow of product throughout Europe. The bank debt is approaching £2m and there are VAT and income tax payments overdue so there will be additional monies owed once the Group goes into administration.' Phil leaned back in his chair and looked at the ceiling. As though thinking aloud he went on. 'You could continue to run the Elite salons, but the AmDesigns brand is essentially worthless. My recommendation is we play the VA card straight up, stand back and leave the rest to the Administrator. It's the cleanest way and you can start up again when the dust settles.' Having said his piece, Jones put his pen down and waited for the explosion he expected from Amy.

To his astonishment, all she said was, 'you're right. I came to the same conclusion when Peter left for work this morning. Starting over is the best I can hope for.' Amy Speight started to cry.

She cancelled her hotel, deciding to get the train back to Manchester after the meeting with the banks. As there was nothing to discuss or argue about, the meeting had finished by 7.15. The administration of her beloved group of companies was put in train and all she had to do was assist where requested and let events take their course.

Personally, she would be able to tide herself over for about six months. She had money in the bank and some savings. A lot would depend on if or when Peter would sell the house. She wouldn't cut her nose off to spite her face, so she would continue to live there for a while, but she would rent a place of her own as soon as practical. She hoped that this would help her get over the hurt and betrayal that was eating her up inside.

The next three months seemed to fly by. She provided all the help and information she could to the liquidation of her companies, but by Christmas 2009, the need for her involvement had come to a natural end. The process would continue for some time into the New Year, but she was positive that following this she could start over.

There had been limited contact from Peter. He hadn't shown any concern or support; just a couple of phone calls to see how she was and more recently the odd email, the last one saying he'd arranged for an agent to put the house on the market in the new year. This was a positive in Amy's eyes as it would force her to find somewhere else and along with looking for a job, she could get herself back into circulation.

True to his word, Peter arranged for the estate agent to call round on 2nd January and as he breezed around the house cooing at how lovely each room was and saying there would be lots of interest, Amy sat at the kitchen table listing the money she had in her various accounts and going through a box of papers she'd found in her back bedroom office. There was nothing of particular interest in it, until she came to an official looking document near the bottom. She started to smile as she read through it. It was a life assurance policy in her name for £5m, which she'd taken out when the business was booming. As she read the small print, Amy Speight knew that 2010 was going to be a very good year.

Chapter 10

Gray left the meeting with a pack of papers in an A3 envelope. They included two copies of the job offer and his contract signed by Bobby Dulac. A confidentiality agreement which was emphatic about not disclosing any of the company's activities to anyone and a brochure describing the details of the Horizon Life Settlement Fund. Henry was not surprised that he was employed by Horizon Settlement Inc., which was based in the Cayman Islands.

Mignemi and Dulac ordered another coffee after Gray had gone for his train. 'I think he will fit in nicely,' said Dulac. 'And you are confident that that he won't have any issues if things get extreme?'

'It is my belief he was responsible for the death of Mike Jones,' replied Mignemi. 'It can't be proved, but my contacts tell me there is considerable doubt in the Police that it was just an accident. I don't think we will have to use this, but it's always useful to have some insurance.' He smiled at what he thought was a reasonable attempt at humour. 'How is the pipeline of business building for when we launch?'

'It's on track as per the projections. And we've also cleaned the regulatory capital through Luxemburg, so our associates are as happy as they can be,' replied Dulac.

'Good, I'll leave you to get Gray settled in, but let me know if there are any issues or delays.'

When Henry got home, Carol could not get passed the £100k tax free bonus. She didn't really listen to anything else Henry said, and by the time they went to bed, she had them moving to a big house in Brentwood.

Gray's mind was also racing, focusing on how on earth he was going to tell John Harding he was leaving and only giving five weeks of his six month notice period. Dulac had told him almost word for word how to position it, but nonetheless he doubted it would be a pleasant experience.

He got into work a little earlier than usual as he needed to sort out a couple of things, should Harding take his bat home and put him on gardening leave immediately. He knew that Harding always got in early, so went down to his office knocking on the open door and going straight in.

'Henry, what can I do for you?'

'I've been offered another job, with a new start up fund and I feel it's an opportunity that I should take. I really appreciate all the help you've given me John, but I'm ambitious and hopefully you'll understand.'

'Oh,' said Harding, 'now let's not be hasty Henry. You are a key man in this business, so if its more money you're looking for, I'm sure we can sort something out.' His tone was friendly but Gray could see he was struggling to keep it that way.

'It's not about money John. It's a challenge in a different sector that CAM doesn't operate in. Also, the article in FMJ really upset me and I think it's best for everyone that I leave and try and put all that behind me.' Dulac had been insistent that he mention the Justin Kell article specifically. He and Mignemi had clearly done their homework on Henry Gray, but like him they thought the comments about Henry and Mike Jones were unfair. He felt it important to get Harding to understand it would also be good for CAM if he left.

'I understand all that,' responded the CEO, his tone hardening with every word. 'But I've stood by you through all this and that deserves a little loyalty, don't you think!'

Gray didn't flinch. 'I will work until the end of July, if you want me to. The company I'm going to will buy out my contract if necessary. I am grateful for the opportunity you gave me John, but it's my career and this move will be good for me.'

Henry Gary put his resignation letter on Harding's desk and stood to leave.

'Close out any open positions, clear your desk and be out of this office by 9.00am. You are on gardening leave with immediate effect. HR will confirm the details by close of business including the restricted covenants that we will be holding you too. Now get out of my office,' screamed Harding.

Gray couldn't help but smile as he packed up the few personal belongings from his desk. The rest of the staff were still coming in or chatting in the kitchen or coffee area, so no one noticed when he walked out to the lifts. It couldn't have gone any better. He knew how Harding would react and now he had a few weeks off before starting with Horizon. He'd call Dulac when he got home and leave it to him to smooth things over with Harding.

John Harding wished he hadn't reacted in such a hot-headed manner. It was pretty standard practice to put staff with confidential and client information on gardening leave, but to do it in such an unprofessional way made him feel ashamed of how he'd treated Henry. The big headache he had now was recruiting another fund manager and in the meantime he'd have to ask Tim to cover both funds which wasn't ideal. He decided that once he had the details of where Henry was going and provided there was no cross over, he'd negotiate a suitable settlement to let him start there in August.

The next few weeks flew by for Gray. Once Dulac had smoothed things over with Harding, it was clear he expected Henry to start familiarising himself with everything there was to know about the Horizon Life Settlement Fund. The office was in Ely Place, Farringdon, and by the time he officially started on Monday 3rd August 2009, he had a good understanding of the operation together with a lot of questions on things that didn't look or feel quite right.

Regulatory approval from the FCA was expected in the next couple of weeks and the list of individuals who were in the process of selling their policy to Horizon ran to nearly five hundred names with a total value of over $50m. It was like a well-oiled production line as sale agreements were processed, bank transfers made to sellers and prospectuses sent out to interested investors.

The business was clearly well capitalised as there were a couple of dozen people on the payroll and the fund itself wouldn't be making any serious money for at least six months. There was also a significant amount of money going out to the poor souls who had sold them their policy. When Gray asked Dulac about this, he got the same straight bat, 'Our associates who own the business are backing the fund as they see significant growth potential.' Gray was not privy to who these "associates" actually were and the FD and Compliance Director did not share any details of the capital supporting the business.

For Gray to do his job, he needed assets to manage and for this to happen Horizon needed people to die and the death benefit to be paid to Horizon. He didn't scrutinise the details of the sales or the state of health of the sellers, most of whom were American, but he felt it was a bit "hit and miss" for a business to rely on the timings of people's death to make its money. What surprised him even more was that Dulac appeared in no way concerned about the mortality of the lives assured. So when the first few notifications started to come through in the Autumn and this turned to a steady flow by Christmas, Dulac just carried on as though nothing had changed, which did not surprise Henry Gray one bit.

He finally had some assets to manage and interest in the fund was growing, leading to a string of new investors every month, attracted by the promised high yield and diversification into a new and different asset class. All thoughts of Mike Jones and Justin Kell were forgotten as Henry Gray got on with his job and started to enjoy his new found wealth.

Chapter 11

Henry Gray might have forgotten about Justin Kell, but Justin Kell had not forgotten about Henry Gray.

The fund management community was the same as any other. Whether it was genuine news, idle speculation or just plain gossip, it spread quickly and like the game of Chinese Whispers, by the time it had gone full circle there were a number of versions of 'the truth.'

Henry Gray leaving CAM was of course fact. But the reasons for his swift departure ranged from a physical bust up with John Harding to being unable to cope with the death of Mike Jones. That it came so soon after the article in FMJ fuelled the rumour mill regarding Gray's link with the climbing tragedy.

Kell didn't pay any attention to this speculation, but he was very interested to find out the reasons for Gray's leaving and where he had gone. A call to John Harding was not returned and Gray's colleagues at CAM were equally in the dark about Gray's disappearance. Kell surmised that Gray would be remaining in the industry, so all he had to do was keep checking the FCA register to see which firm he went to and Gray's LinkedIn profile which he would be sure to update.

It was early August when Gray updated his LinkedIn details to show his employer as the Horizon Settlement Fund and the following week his FCA registration confirmed him as a fund manager there. Priding himself as knowing the movers and shakers in the industry, Kell was surprised that he had never heard of Horizon or Robert Dulac the CEO; of course, this was easily remedied and at the same time he could shake Henry Gray's tree as well.

Kell was familiar with Life Settlement Funds; they were growing in popularity in the States, but many industry experts were sceptical about their long term viability and regarded them as high risk. His research of the main firms in this sector did not find any mention of Dulac and the details of his other business interests were sketchy. Once he'd exhausted the information that was in the public domain, Kell picked up the phone and went route one.

'Hi, this is Justin Kell from the Fund Management Journal, please could I speak to Robert Dulac?' The receptionist's response was standard. 'What is it concerning, please?'

'I'm doing an article on Life Settlement Funds and was hoping to include Horizon, especially as you are new to the city,' replied Kell.

'Mr Dulac is in meetings all day. If you can leave me your number, I will get him to call you back.'

Kell left his number and decided to give it a few days to see if Dulac got in touch.

Later that afternoon, Dulac was going through his messages and smiled when he saw that Justin Kell had been trying to get hold of him. He used the burner phone to call Mignemi.

'I've had a call from Justin Kell from FMJ saying he wants to do an article on our fund, but I expect he's more interested in Henry. How do you want me to play it?'

'Interesting,' replied Mignemi. 'There is no reason not to be open with him and it may help us to keep Henry close if he puts two and two together and actually makes four. Arrange to see him at the office and make sure Henry knows he's coming. Clearly Mr Kell does not believe that Jones' death was an accident.' With that the call was ended.

Dulac's secretary made the arrangements for Kell to come into the office the following Monday morning at 10.00am, immediately after the weekly meeting.

Gray didn't understand the need for the Monday morning briefing. The management team got together and gave an update on what was on their agenda for the coming week and any issues they were dealing with. Dulac believed it was a good discipline and helped communication throughout the office and it was only half an hour out of everyone's week. Dulac was just bringing the meeting to a close when his secretary came into the meeting room. 'Justin Kell is here for your ten o'clock meeting.'

'Thanks,' said Dulac. 'Put him in my office. I'll be there in a minute.'

Gray felt like he'd been hit in the stomach by a charging bull and didn't hear Dulac wind up the meeting with his usual rallying cry for everyone to work even harder. *What was the scumbag reporter doing meeting with Bobby?* He was in such a daze that he didn't realise that everyone else had left the room. Trying to get his brain engaged to think what this meant, he went back to his desk in the dealing room.

After the opening pleasantries, Dulac asked. 'So Justin what can I do for you?'

'As you are one of the first Life Settlement Funds to be managed here in London, I thought I could give you some free publicity in an article I'm doing on the sector, from their origins in the States, their rapid growth and how you see their future as a viable asset class. But I'd like to start with a short bio of you. University, career history and all that.'

'This firm is not about me, it's about the great people we've got working in it.' Responded Dulac, avoiding answering the question directly. 'I've worked overseas all my life, mainly in the Far East, and I see our fund delivering a good return for investors in addition to helping people who have fallen on hard times.'

Kell did not want to press on the details of Dulac's career at this point, so picked on the concept of '*helping people who have fallen on hard times.*'

'How do you identify people who may want to sell you their life policy for a fraction of what it's worth.'

Ignoring the jibe, Dulac continued with what was clearly a pre-set sales pitch. He talked about the advertising being localised and not national, the power of referrals from people they'd helped and a growing awareness that when payments were missed, there were firms like Horizon who'd pay off the arrears and then buy the policy to provide the necessary cash to those who needed it.

Kell was aware of all this but showed his interest by nodding and smiling until Dulac's annoying American accent finally stopped assaulting his ears. 'Is there anything else you need as I've got another meeting in five minutes,' said Dulac, indicating that the meeting was over.

'Just one more thing,' Kell said. 'How is Henry Gray settling in?'

Dulac beamed, 'he's doing a great job, a really great job, we were lucky he chose us.' With that Dulac stood and held out his hand to close the meeting.

Later that morning, Dulac's secretary buzzed through on Gray's phone. 'Bobby would like to see you in his office as soon as possible.'

He logged out of the various systems he was using and walked down to Dulac's office. The door was open.

'Please shut the door and take and seat.' Dulac's tone was pleasant but not warm. 'I've just had a meeting with Justin Kell from FMJ. I think you guys have met?'

'Yes we have,' replied Henry. 'What did he want?'

'He thinks you are responsible for the death of Mike Jones.' Dulac's tone was ice cold as he stared at an extremely worried Henry Gray.

Chapter 12

JJ locked up the gym and the changing rooms and headed out of the entrance to the sports block. It was 4.30 pm Friday afternoon and he was off to Declans for his weekly medication. It was a couple of weeks since Mike had dropped the bombshell of his crazy plan to make 'them' rich again and JJ was pleased that it hadn't caused him to slip any further into the mist of drink and drugs.

He sat at his usual seat at the end of the bar and the bartender poured him his first shot of the week and left the bottle as usual. Despite his self-perceived abstemious behaviour during the week, he realised the basic economics of his situation could not continue for long. His outgoings exceeded his income and very soon something would have to go. Even when he gave this some sober thought, he knew in his heart that it wouldn't be his medication and that was a big, big problem.

He was musing this over when a familiar voice said, 'Allow me,' and refilled his glass.

He turned to see Mike Sloan standing at the bar with another guy in a sharp blue suit, which seemed ridiculously out of place in Declans.

'Don't be angry JJ, I've come to apologise,' said Mike, sounding like he almost meant it. 'Can we join you?' he gestured to the sharp blue suit, in a needless confirmation that the two of them were together.

'Sure, why not,' replied JJ.

'Let's go and sit at that table in the corner,' said Mike picking up the bottle and the two extra glasses the barman had put down.

When they were settled, Mike introduced blue pin stripe. 'This is Patrick John, he works for a company called Horizon and they are interested in buying that policy we talked about off you.'

'You never give up do you Mike,' JJ responded wearily. 'I thought I had to be a hopeless alcoholic or druggy to satisfy the conditions for sale.' Sharp blue suit stepped in before Mike could respond.

'JJ, my company is different from the rest who operate in this sector. We are only concerned with everyone getting a great deal and because we have a long-term strategy, we are always interested in seeing if we can help people like yourself, irrespective of age, health and lifestyle.'

Not just sharp, blue suit, JJ thought, *but smooth, sharp blue suit.*

Mike interjected. 'I'm really sorry about the last time we met JJ, I shouldn't have said those things and I was wrong to do so. You are my friend and I am trying to help you. Pat here has a proposal that you might want to consider.'

Smooth, sharp, blue suit continued. 'As I was saying, at Horizon we take a longer term view than our competitors. We balance our portfolio with a mix of an elderly, life impaired profile with standard risk lives like yourself.'

This sounded complete gobbledegook to JJ, and this guy was imposing on his JB time so he cut across his full flow.

'Cut the crap please Pat. How much are you going to give me for my policy and how much will my friend Mike make out of the deal.'

Smooth, smart blue suit continued unperturbed, as though JJ had actually paid him a compliment. 'The price paid will be subject to a medical, that I will arrange and will be free of charge. I've agreed to share my commission with Mike, so this won't affect the money you receive.' Without waiting for JJ to reply, he pulled some papers from a briefcase that JJ hadn't even noticed and was laying them on the table as he continued. 'If you could just sign these three forms where JJ is indicated, we can get things moving. The first one is giving us your consent to contact the life company to get the details of the policy, including if the premiums are up to date. 'This one,' he said gesturing to the second form, 'is agreement to undertake the medical and lists the tests that the doctor will undertake. And finally, if you could complete the details of the account you want the money to go into and sign this one.'

'Whoa,' exclaimed JJ. 'Just slow it down Pat!' I need to give this some serious thought. JJ glared at Mike, who was looking as though he'd lost a dollar and found a dime. 'I don't know if I want to get into all this right now and I'm certainly not signing my life away.'

Smooth as ever, blue suit continued. 'By signing these papers you aren't committing to anything JJ. You can back out at any time, even when we give you the final quote. Until then, this just gets the process rolling.'

It took another forty five minutes and the ordering of another bottle of JB, before JJ signed the papers. In the end, he did it just to get rid of them, and of course his "friend" Mike left with the suit, leaving him to enjoy his stupor all alone.

Chapter 13

'He thinks what,' exclaimed Gray.

Dulac repeated his opening statement. 'He thinks you are responsible for the death of Mike Jones.'

Gray sat down in the chair opposite Dulac's desk. 'What did he say? He can't just go around accusing me of murder. It was an accident, that was the Coroner's verdict.' Gray realised he was rambling and made a conscious effort to pull himself together and just sat there staring at Dulac's desk.

Dulac eventually broke the silence. 'We were aware of the incident when Mr Mignemi approached you about working here. In fact, it was one of the reasons that we did. The beauty of the situation is that you are the only person who will ever know the truth of what actually happened that fateful day, so whilst we may concur with Kell's view, it does not change our opinion that you are a valuable member of staff.'

Gray could not believe what he was hearing. Did his boss just say the *beauty of the situation* and refer to him as *valuable* like he was an asset in their fund? His instincts told him that the next twenty or so minutes were going to be critical for his entire future so he decided to let Dulac do the talking and see what was really going on. 'What exactly are you saying Bobby?'

'My associates who back this operation like to remove any risk that their business interests are exposed to. If Kell wants to dig the dirt on you, then it's likely he will also look into our operation, which is something that simply must not happen. So my British friend, we have a problem and its one that you will be sorting out.'

As though it was perfectly choreographed, at that very moment Mignemi walked into Dulac's office. There was an imperceptible nod between them that Gray didn't notice as Mignemi pulled a chair from the meeting table over to the desk.

He spoke in his usual crisp and unemotional manner. 'You will remove the problem of Mr Kell, Henry, and as we like to reward our employees for their loyalty and complete discretion, you will be promoted to the Board. As a sign of good faith, this will happen immediately. Robert has a new contract for you with all the details, including revised salary and bonus arrangements. We appreciate what we are asking you to do takes time, but we expect resolution by the end of the year. We will not speak about this matter again, unless there is a problem that requires my input. By signing your new contract you are agreeing to these terms.'

Dulac had produced the papers from his desk drawer and pushed them towards Gray. 'There's no need to read them Henry, it basically says you are one of us now.'

Henry was stunned. He felt threatened, frightened and elated at the same time. His mind could not focus, he could not speak and his heart was beating so fast he felt it would burst from his chest. He simply sat in stunned silence.

'Henry, do you understand everything Mr Mignemi has said. We need your decision right now.' Dulac said.

'Of course,' stammered Henry, taking his pen from his inside pocket. He signed the two copies of the new contract and pushed them back across the desk.

Dulac picked them up and handed one copy back, 'This one is yours,' he smiled.

'Now let's get back to business,' said Mignemi. 'We are attracting the wrong type of clients and we need to improve the return from our assets. Robert, please run through your ideas so Henry is up to speed.

Justin Kell had not gained any further insight into Bobby Dulac following their meeting other than he didn't like the guy. The whole set up felt wrong somehow but right now he didn't have the time to go chasing what could be a red herring. He would keep a close eye on developments at Horizon and defer any article on Life Settlement Funds. There was a plethora of stories he was pursing due to the ongoing financial crisis and it was also time for his six monthly psyche evaluation, which was a hangover from his time when he was undercover in the Met and that fateful last assignment.

They moved from Dulac's office into the Boardroom which indicated the change in subject and made it feel more official. Dulac began, 'Our sales agents in the States are doing a decent job and we receive a steady flow of policies into the fund. The problem is that the sweet spot in the market is in the blue collar sector and this is reflected in the sum assured of the policies. The average is a little over $100k. The other issue is that the cost of the assistance we need to turn these assets into cash is going up, which impacts on the bottom line and the amount of clean cash we can remove from the business. So I've got two recommendations; one, we start to target Europe for suitable clients and secondly we bring the assistance regime in house.'

Gray couldn't help himself, he just had to ask the question he already knew the answer to. 'Just so I'm clear, what exactly is the assistance regime?'

It was Mignemi who answered. 'Our competitors in this sector are struggling with liquidity issues. Put simply, the people whose policies they've bought are living longer than expected. We anticipated this, prior to entering the market, so made arrangements with a third party, you could call it outsourcing, to ensure that our fund did not have this problem. Accidents happen all the time Henry, and in the poorer areas of certain States in the US this is not uncommon. Our main concern is that if anyone were to pick up on the trend…'

'Such as an investigative journalist,' said Gray.

'Indeed, such as an investigative journalist,' continued Mignemi, 'then we would need to address this promptly.'

Dulac took over. 'The proposal is we target clients who have significantly higher value policies. There are a lot of business people struggling with the recession that's hitting here and the States right now. Our plan is to identify such individuals and give them the opportunity to sell us any policies they may have.'

Gray's confidence was growing so he again interjected. 'The only problem with this is that the age and health profile will be such that the return could be twenty or thirty years down the road and with us paying the premiums, our cash flow will be screwed…'

It was at this precise moment that Henry Gray realised that the day Mike Jones fell to his death while rock climbing had sucked him into a life he'd only ever read about in books.

'I think the penny has finally dropped with Henry,' Mignemi said to Dulac. 'I will start to make the arrangements to end our third party agreement and move the assistance we need in house. Robert, I will leave it to you and Henry to change our focus to higher value policies and suggest we meet again in a couple of months to review progress.' With that, Mignemi got up and left the room.

Gray looked at Dulac, wondering how on earth he could get himself out of this complete and utter mess.

Chapter 14

The estate agent was right. There was a lot of interest in Peter's house and within a week of it going on the market a sale had been agreed to a couple who were first time buyers. With no chain, the sale would go through in about eight weeks.

Amy had never been busier. She had a string of interviews lined up for jobs that she was actually interested in, she was checking out suitable flats and she had a meeting with Phil Jones who was technically still her accountant and was always available to give a helping hand and advice on her finances.

At the top of her list of priorities was getting a job. Once she had some money coming in, she could start to make plans and it would also determine the type of apartment she could afford to rent. The job interviews she'd had so far had not gone as she'd expected. Her CV was clear on who she was, the success she'd achieved and the humiliation of her empire crumbling from within and going into liquidation. So she was surprised when prospective employers interviewed her that they all thought she would only stay with them for a few months and then move onto something bigger and better or that she was out to take their job as she steamrollered her way to the top. When she had been turned down for the third time, she realised she needed to change her approach and get on the front foot.

Today's interview was with a technology company, whose head office was in London and who ran their admin and marketing from an office on the outskirts of Manchester. They were looking for a Brand & Marketing Director and Amy felt she was perfect for the job.

The interview was with the MD and head of HR who had travelled up from London and the first thing that surprised Amy when she walked into the interview room was how young they were. After the opening pleasantries, Amy took the lead.

'Before we start you will see from my CV that I built my own group of companies from scratch and grew them significantly to become a major global brand. On that journey, I worked in every department of the business and knew all my staff by their first names. When the group went into liquidation, I worked tirelessly to ensure my staff were well treated and helped the majority of them find other jobs. I'm here today because I want to help you grow your business and build a brand that is recognised internationally. I do not want to take over the company and I'm not using you to get my career back on track, just to leave in six months when something better comes along. I am loyal and committed, so I'd be grateful if you would bear this in mind throughout the interview.'

Amy smiled and waited for the first question.

It was Mark Peters the MD who spoke first.

'Thank you, Amy, but there is not going to be an interview.'

Amy was stunned into silence as she realised her "great idea" had backfired. All she could manage was, 'oh, I see.'

Mark Peters stood and held out his hand. 'I'd like to offer you the job.' Nodding toward the HR Director, he continued. 'Marie will run through the terms and the pay and rations and I'd like to see you before you leave.'

'But why, I don't understand,' stammered Amy.

'I'm very aware of who you are and what you achieved. You have all the skills we are looking for and the Board want someone with the energy, vision and creativity to build our brand over the next five years. Your opening statement told me everything I need to know about you Amy. I actually hope that you will take my job eventually because that means we will all be successful. I also know you won't leave as this is a great place to work and we only employ the best people. Now if you'll excuse me, I'll leave you with Marie and I'll see you before you leave.'

As she walked out into a dreary late February day, Amy Speight was on cloud nine. The terms that Marie had run through with her were fabulous. They'd signed everything there and then and she started a week on Monday. Her thoughts now turned to reconsidering the apartments she would be able to afford. There were some very nice ones in the Castlefield area of the city which would be handy for the tram to get her out to the office and still central enough to be close to the bars and restaurants in the centre. Amy checked her watch. It was just coming up to eleven o clock so she had plenty of time to pop into the estate agents and arrange some viewings for later on in the week, before she met Phil Jones for lunch.

It was no surprise when she walked into Evuna on Deansgate that she saw her accountant already sitting at the table in the corner at the back of the restaurant. She was only ten minutes late which was basically on time in her mind.

'Hi Phil, sorry I'm late,' she beamed.

'No problem, I've only just got here myself. What would you like to drink?'

'I think I'll have a glass of Cava please, as finally I've got something to celebrate!'

'Great,' replied Phil. 'I can't join you as I've got a client meeting straight after this. So just soft drinks for me.'

The waiter came over with the usual bottle of water and a couple of chunky glasses and they ordered their drinks.

'Now tell me what it is you're celebrating and then I've got some other good news for you as well,' said Phil.

Amy had just got started recounting the unusual interview she'd had earlier that day when the waiter appeared for their order. They settled on the lunchtime special, which was a selection of tapas which included a glass of house wine.

Amy recounted the interview virtually word for word, getting more and more animated as she finished her Cava and started on the wine. By the time she'd finished, they'd polished off most of the food and she had drunk Phil's wine as well!

When Amy clearly had no more to say, Phil saw his opportunity to share his news before he had to dash off to his client meeting.

'That's fabulous Amy, it's great that you've got yourself sorted. New job, new apartment and a potential windfall on the way.'

'Ooh, that sounds exciting,' said Amy, 'what's all that about then.'

Phil continued, 'you know that life policy that you've got from when you set up the business. Well, I was talking to a friend of mine who arranged to sell a similar policy for a client of his to this firm based in London. They buy policies for a small percentage of the sum assured, you know, the amount that gets paid out when the policy holder dies. They take over paying the premiums and get the money when you eventually croak.'

'How much would they pay?' Amy's head quickly clearing from the alcohol buzz at the mention of money.

'Their market is normally older people in poor health, but this firm is taking a long term view and want a proportion of longer term assets in their fund. This firm has a strong base in the US but are starting to look at the European market as they expand. I think you may get between 5% and 10% of the sum assured, so being conservative about £250,000.'

'I don't see the need for the policy now that I've no business and I'm on my own. But with such an amount, I could forget renting and actually buy a place! It sounds almost too good to be true, so what's the catch?'

'There's no catch as far as I can tell. The firm is registered with the FCA and I spoke to the MD and discussed your situation in general terms, keeping your name anonymous of course. They don't have any agents in the UK yet, so he said he'd be happy to arrange to meet you himself.'

'OK great, I can't see any harm in a meeting. What's his name?'

Phil replied, 'Bobby Dulac from the Horizon Life Settlement Fund. I'll make the arrangements for the three of us to meet next week.'

Chapter 15

Gray's biggest problem was that he couldn't discuss his dilemma with anyone. After the meeting with Dulac and Mignemi, he'd left the office early and headed back to Essex. Instead of going home, he went to small pub near the station where he knew he wouldn't be recognised to try and absorb the day's events.

On the positive side, he was now a director at Horizon and the pay rise was huge. Carol would be delighted and she would be able to start seriously looking for the big house in Brentwood. So that box was ticked.

After that, he was struggling. Ok, he was a fund manager in the city of London and very well paid but it had come with a huge downside.

Dulac and Mignemi knew he had killed Mike Jones.

This had led them to conclude that he would be capable of murdering Justin Kell and thus end any further speculation and bad press. It would also make sure that the reporter didn't take any further interest in Horizon's activities.

The "associates" who back the Horizon business clearly operate on the wrong side of the line. It appears that money is somehow being laundered through the Group. To ensure the returns on the fund and the cash flow stands up, they arrange for clients who have sold them their life policies to have a premature demise. This ensures Horizon get the proceeds earlier than forecast. Now they were bringing this "in house" which would make him an accessory to a very unsavoury business model. He chuckled to himself thinking, *no big deal as I'm already a cold-hearted killer.*

As he sat there sipping his lager, he realised that this was a complete change of mind set for him. Throughout the Mike Jones incident, he had never really thought of himself as a murderer. Somehow he'd convinced his sub-conscious self that it was an accident. After all he hadn't pulled out a knife and stabbed him, which is what murdering someone was, wasn't it? But he knew that whilst there wasn't any premeditation, he'd had a clear conscious thought of what he was doing when Mike fell to his death. So, if the truth ever got out, there would be only one conclusion – he was a killer.

Gray understood that there were only two courses of action. He and Carol could run away; pack up and leave and try and start again somewhere. The obvious flaw in this was his colleagues would find him and doubtless find a terminal way to ensure his silence. On the other hand, he could accept what he was and was *all in*, accept the risks and enjoy the lifestyle.

Having made his decision, he finished his drink and set off home to tell his wife the great news of his promotion.

The next few months were largely uneventful as Gray continued to manage the fund and it was business as usual. There was no further discussion on any of the matters Dulac and Mignemi had shared with him prior to his promotion and with Carol finding the home of their dreams and a buyer snapping up their place as soon as it went on the market, all was well with the world as Christmas approached. There had been no sign of Justin Kell and no articles in his paper on anything related to Horizon and the problems in the life settlement market. On this basis, Gray didn't feel he needed to give any serious thought to how he could ensure this situation continued, believing he could address it should the matter become pressing.

As the markets were generally quiet over the Christmas period, Gray decided to take a week off which would extend to ten days with the bank holidays. He had his usual one to one meeting scheduled with Dulac that afternoon, where he hoped to get an indication of how much his latest bonus would be.

When he finished up everything he needed to and left the instructions for his assistant while he was away, he walked down to Dulac's office and smiled when he saw a bottle of Bollinger in an ice bucket and a couple of glasses on the desk.

'What are we celebrating?' enquired Gray.

'A great year with some great results,' beamed Dulac pouring two glasses of the fizz. He handed one to Henry. 'Cheers, my friend, thanks for all the hard work and congratulations on a great job running the fund.' They chinked glasses.

'Thanks,' said Henry. 'It's nice to be appreciated.'

'We sure do appreciate you Henry, and we reward those people we appreciate and can rely on.' He pulled a folded sheet of A4 out of his pocket and handed it to his colleague.

Gray put down his glass so he could unfold the paper. As he read the short paragraph, he started to beam from ear to ear. 'Wow, thanks Bobby, I never expected a bonus of this much.'

'Three quarters of a million pounds is nothing to what you can expect going forward if everything comes together,' replied Dulac. 'But there is just one condition before the money gets paid into your account.'

'What's that?'

'You must permanently resolve the problem of Justin Kell.'

'But we haven't heard a peep from him since he came to see you. Surely, he's forgotten about me by now and he's not got any interest in our fund.' Henry Gray was trying not to sound desperate.

'Let me be very clear Henry. As long as you work here, our business is potentially exposed to a greater level of scrutiny, and we simply cannot let that happen. Alfio made it very clear what we expect from you when you got your promotion and you must deliver.'

'I know what we agreed, but I've no idea how to go about planning such an act. I don't know his routine, where he goes, what his hobbies are. In fact, I don't know anything about him.'

Dulac went back to his desk and got a manila folder out of his drawer. 'Everything you need to know about Kell is in here. Where he lives, where he eats, what he does at weekends. He is a man who has his demons from his time in the Met, so it should not be a difficult task. We believe that the best cover is to do these things in a very public place with lots of people about. It needs to look like an accident, so the more witnesses there are, the better.'

Gray just nodded. "OK" was all he managed to say. He turned and walked out of Dulac's office, 'One last thing Henry. This is your number one objective for the first quarter. You got that?'

'Yes, understood and happy Christmas to you too.'

Chapter 16

Justin Kell rang the bell of the Harley Street psychiatrist that he had been seeing for the last five years. In the beginning, he'd found it difficult to discuss what had happened on his last undercover assignment. The events were too shocking to even think about. But with the gentle probing from Mr Bhati, he had slowly began to open up and let out the horrors of those fourteen months that had cost him his wife, his job and almost his life.

In the early days, the sessions with the consultant psychiatrist had been weekly. But as his mind and body slowly began to heal, they gradually became less frequent and were now every six months. He had no idea if they would ever end, but the Force looked after their own and as long as they kept paying, he'd keep turning up for his two hours of therapy which was helping to keep him sane.

They'd stopped talking directly about the operation itself a couple of years ago. In the last few sessions the discussions were more general, covering what he'd been doing, if there had been any incidents that prompted flashbacks and his state of health both physical and mental.

'Justin, good to see you,' Bhati's greeting was as warm and genuine as ever.

'Good to see you too Arjun. How have you been these past six months?'

'Have been very well thank you. But it's not my health that we are here to discuss. Sit down and tell me what you've been up to since we last spoke.'

And as casually as that, the session had begun.

'Work has been pretty much the same as usual. I've written some decent articles and only had a couple of complete mind blanks, which is getting better all the time.'

They'd discussed the "mind blanks" extensively over the years, agreeing early on that it wasn't just writer's block that was happening. At completely random moments, it was as though all conscious thought left Justin Kell's mind. He didn't freeze like a statue as his body, driven by his sub-conscious self, according to the doc, would continue to function, undertaking the chores of the day or continuing to walk, or just typing gibberish on his touch pad. After a period of up to ten minutes, his mind would free itself and he'd be left wondering what had happened. There was never any pre-warning that they were about to happen and despite the good doctor's attempts to identify physical or emotional triggers, five years down the line they were none the wiser to understanding why they occurred.

'Did they occur while you were working?' enquired Bhati.

'Yeh, and within a couple of days of each other. On both occasions, I was drafting an article based on an interview I'd done with a guy called Henry Gray. It was part of a series on boutique fund management firms, but my interest in Gray was piqued following his involvement in the death of one of his colleagues.'

Bhati sat back and just listened as Kell recounted in great detail the Henry Gray story. When he'd finished, Kell realised he had his eyes closed the whole time and when he opened them, he saw the doc sitting impassively jotting notes onto his pad.

'Do you think it is more like an investigation you are undertaking into Mr Gray rather than just writing an article?' asked Bhati.

'Yes, I suppose it was. It's my belief that Gray caused Mike Jones' death either intentionally or accidentally and it's important to me that the truth comes out.'

'How do you feel about this?' prompted Bhati.

'I feel frustrated and angry that there is nothing more I can do about it. It nags away in the back of my mind like a bad headache that's just getting started.'

'Are you sleeping well?'

'Same as usual. I'm not waking up in the middle of the night thinking of Henry Gray if that's what you mean.'

The conversation paused as Bhati made more notes on his pad. When he'd finished, he looked up, 'I think it would help if we went back to the beginning. We still have forty minutes left, so tell me about Operation Checkmate; from day one.'

Kell was not prepared for this shift in the session. He'd recounted the detail of the case on numerous occasions and always felt devastated at how he'd let the operation get out of control. But he knew better than to question the doc's reasoning, so he put his head back, shut his eyes and sent his mind back to August 2003 when the horror story began.

'I'd done a couple of short undercover operations in the early part of 2003. I can't say I'd enjoyed them, but we got the results and the powers that be thought I was good at it. I can clearly remember being called into the Chief Super's office that morning and the smile he welcomed me with before he briefed me on Operation Checkmate.

Back then, people trafficking was rife and just starting to receive regular coverage in the media. I remember being shocked when the Chief told me that there were over 4000 women and children that had been trafficked into the UK in the last twelve months and sold into prostitution. However, despite the growing concerns, this wasn't a matter for the Met as at the time the regional forces had set up specialist units to deal with the problem.'

Kell sighed and shook his head before continuing.

'A lot of traffic was coming through Dover and Folkstone and the intel was that a very senior officer in the Kent Police, was at best turning a blind eye or worst case scenario was running a trafficking syndicate. My brief was to infiltrate the syndicate, gather evidence to identify and convict our bad apple and shut down the operation.'

Although he'd heard the story before, Bhati continued to make notes on his pad as though this was all new to him. 'What were your immediate thoughts when you were given the assignment?'

'How I would tell Tina. She wasn't happy when I went away for just a few weeks on the earlier assignments. The view was that this could take up to twelve months or more, so even with the odd secure meeting at a safe house, we would be losing a year of our life together.'

Kell paused as he relived the moment he told Tina that he would be going undercover for an undetermined period that was likely to be up to twelve months.

'We had the most awful row. She was screaming at me, shouting all sorts of crazy stuff like I didn't love her, why don't I just resign, why did it have to be me and that I shouldn't be surprised if she'd gone when I eventually came home.

'In the end she was right on all counts. I should have said no, walked away and stuff the consequences. Instead, my ego took over and that was that. I only saw her once more after that, at a secure meeting about four months down the line. It didn't last long as all she said was that she was leaving, going to work abroad and that she was sorry that it had ended this way. No recriminations, just very cold and matter of fact.'

Bhati stood up. 'That's our time up today Justin, but I'd like you to come back in a couple of weeks so we can continue with this. Please make an appointment with my secretary on the way out.'

They shook hands and wished each other a happy Christmas and all the best for 2010.

As he walked to the underground, Kell wondered why the doc had wanted to go over the same old ground again. He probably just wants to screw the Met for some more fees and after all he wasn't that bothered about reliving the past, was he?

Chapter 17

In the early part of 2010, Henry Gray was not quite himself. He was just about maintaining equilibrium at work when he had the focus of managing the Horizon Settlement Fund, but outside of this, his mind consistently reverted to the problem of Justin Kell. He had read the dossier that Dulac had provided which did provide a greater insight into Kell's movements, habits, bars and restaurants he regularly visited and the gym he frequented, but it didn't help in any way with how he could do what was being asked of him. No more had been said on the subject but he knew better than to expect that the problem had simply been forgotten about.

It was a bleak end of winter day at the end of February when Dulac walked into the dealing room and Gray was surprised to see Mignemi with him. It was gone 6.00 pm and the rest of the staff had left for the day; with their privacy ensured, his colleagues pulled up a couple of chairs to his desk and as per the norm, Mignemi got straight to the point.

'We are about to acquire a significant asset from our agent in the US. He is exactly what we are looking for. An ex NFL player with a history of drink and drug problems. Thirty three years old with a $10m policy with an annual premium that is now overdue. He signed the consent forms yesterday and will have our medical next week. We will offer $950k and he will accept because his life is slowly disappearing into a bottle of liquor. Our intention is to realise this asset in the next six months and process the money through the fund. Henry, you will need to consider how to manage the FCA reporting requirements and what will be the best time for the credit to hit the fund. I assume it would be immediately following the end of June reporting period but we will take your advice. Please let Robert know when you have determined this and he will arrange for the realisation of the asset at the appropriate time. Any questions?'

'Who is the client?' asked Gray.

It was Dulac who replied, 'A guy named JJ Carmichael. Had a couple of great seasons in the NFL but got hit by a bad injury. Now works as a janitor in the local high school and drinks his weekends away in his local bar.'

'How can you ensure the timing of the er "realisation" of the asset?' Gray couldn't bring himself to say killing or murder.

'Our guy over there has a 100% record. No mistakes. It will look like an accident as usual, but as this guy is a minor celebrity, we expect more than the usual police attention and it will be our first case that hits the national press, but the reward outweighs the risks.'

Mignemi took over. 'Once the money has hit the fund, you will remove it over six months to various overseas accounts. I will provide you with the details at the appropriate time. By the time we have to do our next reports nobody will be any the wiser.'

'If there's no more questions Henry, Alfio and I have a meeting to get to. Suggest we catch up in the morning.'

Henry put his head in his hands and wondered how his life had come to this. Was it just because of a crazy moment rock climbing in Bristol or was it because he was stupid and greedy. He was in way over his head and whilst he had previously convinced himself he was "all in", right now, he would give anything for being as far "out" of this shit storm as possible.

There was no one he could turn to. He'd discounted going to the police on numerous occasions. He would lose his job, probably end up in jail and that was only if his employers didn't "realise" him first. He couldn't disappear with or without Carol. She wouldn't leave her newly acquired dream home and he didn't have enough cash to last more than a few months as it had all gone into the new house.

Later that evening, as he sat on the train heading home, sipping his first class gin and tonic, he had the craziest thought. Maybe just maybe there was someone who could help him and he could kill two birds with one stone.

Chapter 18

It was the start of another week and Amy Speight felt like she had never been busier. Even when her old company was at the peak of its growth and she had been working sixteen hour days just to stand still, it hadn't felt like the last few weeks.

She'd started her new job and had made her first priority to get a detailed understanding of a product range and service offering that was alien to her. If she was going to be able to successfully market the technology solutions that her new firm offered, she had to be able to understand them inside out. She had endless meetings with the developers; she was up and down to London at least once a week and she was assessing her staff to see if they could cut it and would buy in to Amy's vision for the brand and its marketing.

She'd found an apartment that she wanted to buy, which was conditional upon her getting the money from her life policy. Phil Jones had arranged the meeting with Bobby Dulac for Thursday evening in London, which coincided with one of her London days.

Things were full on in Amy's life and that was just the way she liked it.

Thursday came, and Amy was booked on the 6.20 am train out of Manchester Piccadilly. Assuming no delays this would just about get her to her first meeting at 9.00 am. She was then in back to back meetings all day, including a working lunch and had to get into the West End for 6.30 pm for her meeting with Bobby Dulac. She couldn't stay over as she needed to get back North that night as she had a meeting first thing Friday morning in Manchester. This would mean another very long day.

Phil Jones had arranged for them to meet with Dulac at a small bistro he knew in Covent Garden. He booked a quiet table at the back of the restaurant so they wouldn't be overheard. Jones expected that Amy would be running late but viewed this as an opportunity for him to meet with Dulac alone and get the measure of the man.

Phil Jones was a conservative kind of guy. Not a traditionalist but he knew how things should be done and the behaviour expected of him when meeting clients and generally how to conduct oneself. He thought himself a good judge of character.

His first impression of Bobby Dulac was one of a typically bold and brash American and someone that he wouldn't trust as far as he could throw him.

As the waiter showed Dulac across to the table where Jones was already seated, he saw a man in his mid-forties in a sharp suit, plenty of jewellery on display on his fingers and wrists, slicked back black hair with a touch of grey at the temples and an arrogance that could match a Hollywood A lister.

'You must be Phil,' drawled Dulac. 'I'm Robert Dulac, but most people just call me Bobby. The pretty lady not here yet,' he said looking around the restaurant.

'Clearly not,' replied Phil. 'She's running a little late but should be here soon. What would you like to drink?'

In the ten minutes before Amy arrived, it wasn't so much of a conversation between Jones and Dulac as the American basically talked about himself and the opportunities in the life settlement market. Jones did not get the chance to ask the questions he wanted of Dulac, particularly the specifics of his background, how the fund was capitalised and the profile of investors who were investing in it. After all, he was always interested in hearing about new investment opportunities for his clients.

When Amy finally arrived, Dulac effortlessly shifted his tack putting all his focus on the prospective client.

'Sorry I'm late,' said Amy. 'My last meeting ran over and the tube was horrendous.'

'No need to apologise; I'm Bobby Dulac and you of course are Amy Speight.'

Amy held out her hand expecting the formality of a handshake, so she was taken aback when Dulac leaned forward and gently kissed it.

'Very pleased to meet you,' drawled Dulac. 'I'm sure we will work well together.'

Blushing slightly, Amy took her seat and the waiter brought the menus over for them to peruse. Dulac was charm itself. He seemed not to take his eyes off Amy as he asked her about where she was working, how the business was going, what she liked doing in her spare time including the holidays she'd been on.

Jones could see that Amy was lapping it all up and enjoying the attention, so decided it was time to get down to business. 'So tell us Bobby, why should we be talking to you about selling Amy's policy?'

Clearly resenting the interruption, Dulac replied. 'Let's leave that till after we've finished eating; I'm enjoying this lovely lady's company so much it would be rude to spoil the moment by talking shop.'

Jones felt he had well and truly been put back in his box so excused himself and headed for the washrooms. When he returned, another bottle of wine had been ordered and he could see that Amy was getting just a little bit tipsy.

Fortunately, no one wanted dessert so Dulac shifted the conversation to what they were there for originally.

'The Horizon fund is like any other. Anyone can invest in it and the forecast is that returns will exceed those from a FTSE tracker. What makes us different is the assets we invest in. Instead of your usual, bonds, property, stocks and cash, we invest in life policies. It's been a growing asset class in the States in recent years, offering diversification from your standard funds. Quite simply we buy life policies from individuals and take over the payment of the premiums. We pay a percentage on the dollar, which is subject to the mortality rates and a medical that we undertake; which is free of charge of course.'

Dulac paused and smiled as though this was a big deal.

'Our target market is the over sixties, who usually have some health issues. This can get us our return in anything from one to ten years. Right now the fund is doing very well and we are looking for longer term assets to support our capital requirements for the regulator.'

It was Amy who asked the obvious question. 'So how much would you pay me for my policy?'

'You will appreciate that for younger clients the price is considerably less than for our standard market, but I expect it could be up to 5% of the sum assured. This is of course subject to the medical.'

Amy was satisfied with what she had heard, and the potential price was in line with her expectations. She just wanted to get her hands on the money to provide the deposit for her apartment. It was Phil Jones who wanted more detail on how the fund operated and insisted on probing Dulac for the next ten minutes before running out of steam.

Dulac took this in his stride, much to Jones's chagrin. 'If you want to proceed Amy, I'll set up the medical and once this is complete I suggest you come over to our office and we can sign the forms.' It was clear he did not regard Jones as being required for this meeting.

'That's fine with me,' responded Amy. 'We might as well take it to the offer stage before making the final decision. Phil, do you agree?'

'Yes, that makes sense. We can all make the final decision when we next meet Mr Dulac,' replied Jones.

Dulac smiled as he stood up to leave. 'I'll make the arrangements and be in touch.'

When she was sure Dulac had left the restaurant, it was Amy who broke the silence.

'You don't like him do you Phil?

'Was it that obvious. He's a real sleaze ball as far as I'm concerned and I didn't like the way he was clearly chatting you up. Very unprofessional in my opinion.'

'I thought he was quite charming,' said Amy. 'And if he'll buy my policy, I don't care if you think he's a sleazy American'

'The thing is, I can't find out anything substantial about his background. He just appeared in London eighteen months ago as CEO of this Fund Manager. No one had heard of him before which makes me sceptical about all his flannel.' Jones was unerring in is view of Bobby Dulac.

'Look, I appreciate your concerns Phil, but I'm a grown woman and I've dealt with far worse types than Bobby Dulac. Let's get the deal done and then we can forget about him.'

As he headed back to his apartment after the meal with Amy and her accountant, Bobby Dulac had a lot on his mind. He was surprised at how much he had enjoyed her company and was annoyed with himself for taking the flirting so far. Sure, she was an attractive woman and if the circumstances were different, maybe they could take things further. But this could not happen because business was business and Amy Speight was just another asset.

Chapter 19

It had been a rough weekend for JJ Carmichael. He'd been high jacked by his supposed friend Mike Sloan and whilst he wasn't bothered about the money he'd get for his policy, he felt he'd been coerced into signing the papers.

This had required a couple of extra bottles to see him through to Monday morning and as he walked through the High School gates, he felt dreadful and realised if he didn't change his ways soon he might not live to see the term out.

'Hi JJ, how was your weekend?' Sammi Renniker's greeting was full of the energy and bounce that JJ hadn't felt himself for a couple of years.

'OK thanks Sammi, just the usual you know, how about you?'

Sammi Renniker, a sports teacher in the school was in her early thirties and always tied her long blonde hair in a ponytail that swished from side to side whenever she moved her head. This was just about all the time as she never seemed to stay still for longer than a second. She'd caught up to JJ just as they got to the Sports Hall entrance. When she looked at him her shock was real.

'Christ JJ you look terrible, are you sure you're OK?' said Sammi.

JJ sat on the bench facing the football field and put his head in his hands. When he spoke it came through a cascade of tears that made him sound like a small kid trying to say sorry for some terrible misdemeanour.

'Not really, Sammi. In fact, not at all. I'm struggling to cope and I don't know what to do.'

Sammi Renniker did not need to switch into teacher mode. Like all teachers, as soon as she walked through the gates she was full on teachermatic, always ready to sort out issues with the kids and deal with the problems of the day.

'Right, you are coming with me. I'll take you home, make you some breakfast and we can talk this thing out.' The teacher's authority in Sammi's tone left no room for argument.

'I'll ring the Principal and explain you are not well and that I will take the morning to help you out. There won't be any problem arranging cover for any of my lessons.'

JJ didn't have the energy to argue so he stood up and walked to the staff car park where Sammi had parked her Prius.

On the drive to JJ's, they stopped at a grocery store and Sammi picked up some fresh fruit and veg. She didn't have any doubt about JJ's self-medication problem, the smell of his breath and his clothes told her all she needed to know. She also braced herself as they got to the door of JJ's apartment because she knew it would not be pretty inside.

JJ had recovered himself on the drive from school and realised the further humiliation there would be if he let Sammi see the inside of his apartment.

'Thanks Sammi, I'll be alright now. I just need to get some sleep. I'll see you tomorrow at school and thanks for helping me out.' JJ put his in key in door, but there was no way Sammi was going to stop there.

'You might be one of the greatest NFL players of all time JJ Carmichael, but you are not side stepping this one.' She pushed passed his considerable bulk and walked into the apartment.

Despite expecting the place to be a mess, Sammi Renniker had never seen anything like the chaos in the living room which reflected the broken image of JJ's life.

It wasn't just the countless bottles that were strewn everywhere, or the food wrappers or the half eaten take away cartons with the crusted food going rotten. It was the complete sense of despair that pervaded from the room. Not being deterred, she found some room on the dining table for the groceries and braced herself as she inspected the other rooms. The bedroom and bathroom were slightly better but the kitchen was disgusting. Food slops everywhere. The sink overflowing with dirty dishes. Empty bottles of Jim Beam piled in every corner and worse of all the flies.

'You can't stay here JJ. You'll have to come to mine. I'll arrange to get the place cleaned up and you can move back in when you're feeling better. Grab some clothes and let's go.'

Decision made, JJ followed his saviour out of the health hazard of his apartment, just hoping she had some booze in at her place.

Sammi Renniker lived on the other side of town, in a modest neighbourhood, where the neighbours cut their grass and kept their gardens tidy. JJ didn't know anything about the school teacher, but this changed as soon as he went inside the house. Everything was neat and orderly, all the walls painted the same shade of magnolia, a huge bowl of fruit on the kitchen table and not a bottle of booze in sight.

'The bathroom's upstairs on the right; if you go and have a shower JJ, I'll fix you some breakfast.'

JJ did as he was told. When he'd showered and changed into some clothes that didn't smell quite as bad as the ones he'd gone to school in, he came down to find a fruit smoothie on the table and a pot of fresh coffee.

Renniker smiled at him, 'Does that feel better? I made you a smoothie and some coffee. It's decaf of course.'

'Of course,' muttered JJ as he sat down and started sipping his drink.

Renniker sat next to him. 'Do you want to tell me what's wrong JJ?'

'I find it difficult to talk to anyone about it. I've got used to my own company so much that I just have conversations with myself most of the time.' JJ took another sip of the smoothie before switching to the coffee. 'I feel ashamed of what I've become and don't have anyone to turn to.' His eyes never moved from looking at the cup in his hands.

'I'm here for you JJ. You can stay here as long as you like, till you are feeling better. If you want to talk about anything, I'm here to listen. Just one rule,' she looked him in the eye. 'No booze whatsoever. You OK with that?'

'Sure,' muttered JJ, not sounding very convincing to himself, let alone Sammi Renniker.

As the morning went on, JJ began to tell his story. He started at the beginning, when he was playing football in High School, and once he started to talk, he found it surprisingly easy to tell his tale.

Sammi Renniker just listened. She was a good listener and didn't even need to prompt JJ to continue when the emotional parts of the story almost got too much for him. The injury, the divorce, not seeing the kids and the shame of the drinking.

After a couple of hours, JJ was running out of steam, both physically and emotionally. Right on cue, Sammi's phone rang. It was the Principal seeing how things were going and if Sammi would be back in for her afternoon classes.

When she finished the call, she gave JJ a cautious look. 'I'm going back in now. There isn't anyone to cover my post lunch classes. Will you be OK on your own? I'll be back by 4.30 and we can talk more then, if you want?'

'I'll be fine,' said JJ, actually believing himself. 'I need to get some sleep and I promise I'll stay indoors.' It had already been made clear there was no alcohol in the house, so as long as he stayed in, everything should be ok.

Sammi got her bag and headed to the door. 'See you later big guy.' And with that she was gone.

When the door shut behind Sammi, JJ didn't know what to do. He tried to recall the events of the morning to understand how he was sitting in the school teacher's kitchen. It was then that he realised how he was throwing his life down the drain and the hopelessness that had made him believe he could do nothing about it.

He was amazed that a work colleague who he didn't really know had shown such concern for his wellbeing. She was prepared to let him stay in her house and she wanted to help him. Yet, despite these feelings of hope that he hadn't felt for months, he desperately wanted a drink. He stood up and started to systematically go through every cupboard in the kitchen looking for a bottle of something. He knew this was irrational as Sammi had told him that she was teetotal and didn't even have a glass of wine at the weekends.

It was time for JJ Carmichael to make a choice. He could leave the apartment, walk to Declans and start drinking on his tab and the hospitality of the odd local who knew who he had been, or he could stay at Sammi's till she got back. Option one was suicide, option two gave him hope.

Sammi got back from school just after 4.30 as she promised. She found JJ asleep on the couch with the TV playing a daytime quiz show. She smiled as she hung her coat in the closet and went to the kitchen to make some fresh coffee. Just as she was pouring herself a cup, JJ appeared at the doorway. 'Hi Sammi, if that's decaf I sure could do with a cup.'

They chatted about Sammi's afternoon at school and some of the kids who were excelling at sports that JJ knew of before Sammi took the bull by the horns.

'You decided to stay and not go off drinking.' *No point beating about the bush*, thought Sammi.

'Yeh. It wasn't easy. I thought about bolting, but basically, Sammi, you've given me a chance that I know I must take otherwise I'll end up dead in some gutter.'

'Tell me about the drinking, JJ and then we'll see what we can do to make you better.' Sammi's concern for him was palpable. JJ could feel it in her words and see it when he looked into her eyes. 'Just like an AA meeting then,' he joked.

'Yes, just like an AA meeting.' Sammi replied.

They talked long into the night. Sammi made a vegetable casserole which JJ thought was the most delicious food he'd tasted in his life. 'Wow Sammi, I think I wanna be a veggie after that,' beamed JJ.

He helped her clear the dishes and he continued his story at the kitchen table. They agreed not to make any "decisions" on the next steps for JJ until Sammi got back from school the next day. Sammi had cleared with the Principal for JJ to take the week off so they could clean up his apartment and start the process of getting him straightened out.

That week was a struggle for JJ. He spent it at Sammi's house watching daytime TV and going for walks. His mind got clearer by the day and whilst the temptation for a drink burned throughout his body, he managed to stay dry. This was as much for Sammi as for himself.

By Wednesday, he'd agreed to attend a meeting. There was a group that met in a VA Hall not far from JJ's apartment.

By the Saturday, they'd cleaned up his apartment with the help of a local HouseTidy firm, so when they were having a nut roast for Sunday lunch, the realisation that he'd be moving back to what felt like his "old life" was starting to hit home.

JJ was pushing his food around his plate and the conversation that was usually so natural between them was stifled and awkward.

Sammi reached her hand across the table and rested it on JJ's. 'I'd like it if you stayed here until you're completely better JJ. I kinda like having you around.'

'You sure,' replied JJ. 'I'd love to if you mean it. I don't think I can face going back to my place just yet.'

'Of course, I mean it you big oaf!' laughed Sammi. 'We'll get you moved in properly and review the situation at the end of term.'

They stood up and hugged each other as if to seal the deal.

Little did either of them know at that moment that JJ Carmichael would never move back to his old apartment.

Mignemi's burner phone rang. 'Yes.'

'There's a problem with the Carmichael hit. He's cleaned himself up and is living with a teacher from the school. We will need to be more creative to make it look like an accident, which will take time.'

'You have till the end of the month. Just over two weeks is the longest we can wait.'

Mignemi ended the call, picked his other phone and rang the only pre-loaded number.

Chapter 20

'I rented a small house in Alkham, a village between Dover and Folkstone. It was a terrace, what we'd call a two up two down back up North. I had my new ID and had spent the first couple of weeks getting into the routine of visiting the pubs and betting shops that the intel had identified as places of interest that were frequented by the suspected members of the trafficking ring.

'I didn't make contact with anyone, just made sure that my face got seen. I still had a bit of my Manchester accent so the story was I moved south having got out of prison. My rap sheet included pimping prostitutes, GBH and a few other minor offences. This had all been put into the system so anyone checking would believe it was legit.

'After about a month, I was sitting in a pub when one of the key targets came in, a guy known just as Sod. I phoned it in and the plan was a couple of guys on the team would come in and start making trouble with the guy and I'd step in and help him out. I'd take a bit of a beating but hopefully I'd have gained his trust and that would be my in. It all went according to plan until one of our guys got a bit over excited and managed to knock me out with a bar stool intended for Sod's head. They scarpered after that and I was left unconscious on the floor bleeding badly from the side of the head. I woke up in the ambulance and after a night under observation in hospital, I was discharged the following day. The local police interviewed me of course but didn't seem too bothered when I couldn't identify the attackers.

'A couple of days later, I was back in the pub and the landlord said someone wanted to see me in the back. Sure enough, it was Sod and a couple of his sidekicks. Their questioning was a mix of straight talking, mild violence and lots of aggression. I told them my story and that the prison shrink had diagnosed me with "aggressive tendencies" which was why I was always getting involved in every fight that broke out. I told them I was looking for work as a security guard but was struggling to find anything. Being an ex con was not exactly a glowing reference. They let me go and I guessed they would check out my story. It was a couple of weeks later that Sod came up to me in the pub and said he had some work I might be interested in.

'This was the breakthrough as I had made the first step into the periphery of the gang.'

Bhati spoke for the first time since Kell had started talking. 'How did this make you feel?'

'I was excited and scared at the same time. I knew that this was a key step but was very aware that one slip and I'd probably end up dead.

'The operation was beautifully simple. They called the people being trafficked, "cargo". They would usually be in lorries or containers to be loaded onto lorries. We'd go over to Calais and make contact with the drivers. Check that the cargo was in place and give the word to the senior customs guy to wave it through. It was the same on the Dover side. All I had to do was ensure there was no trouble and be on hand if things got a bit messy. Which they did once the cargo was unloaded.

'We'd drive to a small industrial estate a couple of miles into the countryside. All the units were rented by the syndicate and it was there we'd open up the containers.'

Kell paused as he recalled the appalling scenes.

'It was terrible. The appalling state of these poor woman and children. Some had died on the journey and were just lying there. The scenes were so awful, I couldn't believe this was happening in our country.

'The process was to separate the cargo into different groups. The dead were loaded onto a wagon and taken to an incinerator facility that had historically been used to burn diseased cattle. The ones that remained were segregated by age and their state of health. They'd live in the warehouses for a couple of weeks. I was one of the guards who made sure they got fed. They got a new set of clothes and basic toilet facilities were provided. Another crew would eventually come and take them away and then we'd simply repeat the cycle.'

'How did you cope with what you were doing?' enquired Bhati.

'I was on autopilot. I did as instructed and did my best to treat the women with respect. It was the kids that were the worst. Some of them were as young as eight or nine. They were removed from their mum's or whoever they were travelling with and were the first to get shipped out. The looks of hope on their faces when they first got out of the containers was heart breaking; watching it then turn into fear, despair and total grief just about broke me every time.

'After my second run, I managed to meet with the operation's team in a safe house. I told them I wanted out. I couldn't cope with what I was a part of and I wasn't any nearer getting evidence on the ring leaders including any bent coppers. Of course, when you are in that deep, there's no coming out till it's over. The info I'd gathered was useful in building the case, but the focus was to break the syndicate completely and ensure the evidence would convict the chiefs and not just the Indians.

'We got the break just before my third run. Sod had got himself involved in some intense domestic abuse with the woman he was living with. She ended up with a broken arm and jaw and Sod ended up behind bars. I was sitting at the bar in the usual pub when a guy sat on the next stool. I was known as Northy, for the obvious reason.

"Northy, you've been promoted, follow me."

'I later found out that the guy was a sergeant on the Kent force, Dodds was his name. He was the direct link to the top guy, so I was finally making progress.

'I was told I was taking over from Sod as the boss on the ground. Not a lot different to what I'd been doing but I had to get the men in place and organise the contact with the tame Border Control personnel. I'd been instructed to focus solely on the UK side of the operation and now I had some real names of the bastards who were on the payroll.

'It was the third run, where things started to go badly wrong. There were two containers and when we opened them one was completely empty and the other had machine parts. The shit really hit the fan. Somewhere along the line, the containers had been switched or the cargo numbers doctored, and the view was there was a leak in our operation to some rival gang. Being the recently appointed main man on the ground, I was in the firing line.'

There was a long pause as Kell recalled the crude 'interrogation' he was submitted to.

'I had to call it in. I rang Dodds on the emergency number and explained the situation and just over an hour later, four of them appeared, would you believe, in an unmarked police car! They really thought they were untouchable.

'They were convinced it was me. I was chained to an iron ring in the floor of one of the units and beaten with just about anything they could get their hands on. Of course, I didn't have anything to say even if I'd wanted to. They left me there overnight, clearly not bothered whether I lived or died. The next day they returned with one extra in their party. I recognised him immediately. Detective Chief Inspector Doug Smith. He stood away from the main group watching them begin the questioning again. The beating was the same. I could hear my bones breaking as I begged for mercy. When this didn't work, they water boarded me, until I was barely conscious. At this point, Smith walked over and stood over me looking down at my crumpled body.' *"Maybe he doesn't know anything after all. It's a bit of a waste but we can't take any chances. Finish him off and use the incinerator".*

'Those were his exact words. No hint of emotion. No worry. Just another order.

'The next thing all hell broke loose. *"Armed Police, stay where you are. Do not move. Lie on the floor with yours hands over your heads."*

'Then gun shots, screaming and seconds later silence. I'm not sure if I passed out but the next thing I clearly remember was being in the ambulance.'

Although he knew the end of story, Bhati asked. 'What happened at the end Justin.'

'It was Operation Checkmate who had arranged to switch the containers with the intention of drawing out the ringleaders. They decided it was best that I didn't know, so my position would not be compromised. They suspected that Smith was the guy they were after, but again chose not to tell me. They suspected something *might* have gone wrong when I didn't check in after the container had been delivered. They followed Smith and the rest is now history.'

'How did this make you feel Justin?'

'You ask some stupid fucking questions Arjun. I felt betrayed!

'My own colleagues knowingly used me as human bait, I was within minutes of getting killed and they prioritised snaring Smith over my welfare. Later, when I was recovering in hospital it hit me that it wasn't just the feelings of being used and the pain of the treachery of my own colleagues that were ripping me up inside; it was everything else I'd lost. Everything from my "old" life was gone and I wasn't sure I wanted what the future may bring.'

'Did you ever feel suicidal?' asked Bhati.

'Yes and no. I thought about it but knew it was something that I wouldn't be able to do. Maybe I'm just a coward.

'They started my debriefing when I was in hospital, despite the protests from my doctor. When I was discharged a couple of weeks later, we went through it all again. I was told I would be honoured for my bravery in the line of duty and would also get various commendations. I told them to stuff them. I resigned a couple of weeks later and with the help of the Police Federation's solicitor, negotiated an immediate exit but which included pay in lieu of notice for six months and of course access to your good self, Arjun.'

'How do you feel having recounted and relived the events of Operation Checkmate?' asked the doctor.

'On one hand, it seems such a long time ago and yet it also feels just like yesterday. It's not the physical pain I went through or the realisation that I could have died that bothers me. It's the betrayal. I'm not sure I'll ever be able to trust anyone again. But I've told you that before.'

'Our time is just about up, Justin. Thank you for going through it all again. It's my view there will always be some mental scars that you will have to manage but with you getting involved in investigative journalism is likely to prompt flashbacks and potentially the "mind blanks" you have from time to time. You should be aware that the Henry Gray issue was, and is, a trigger in some way to reopening the past. So please be mindful of this if you continue your enquiries.'

'Thanks doc and understood. But I think that story is dead in the water. I'll be focussing on the boring stuff going forward.'

With that they shook hands to confirm the session was over.

As he walked down the steps from the doctor's office onto Harley Street, he glanced across the road and saw a figure he couldn't immediately place crossing the street towards him.

'Hello Justin, I really could do with talking to you,' said Henry Gray.

Chapter 21

Henry Gray had thought long and hard about whether he should approach Kell and if he did how much would he need to tell him to capture his interest. He realised that he couldn't disclose everything about what was going on at Horizon, but it needed to be enough to make Kell start investigating the firm whilst keeping himself at arm's length should matters get out of hand. He needed to get the journalist on his side and should they come to a fork in the road when he'd have to choose sides, then befriending him would help significantly.

Kell's first reaction to seeing Henry Gray crossing Harley Street and walking towards him was initially one of shock. This quickly changed to anger as just minutes ago he'd banished this guy to the depths of his subconscious and now here he was needing to talk to him. What made it worse was he couldn't comprehend how he knew he'd be in Harley Street on this early spring day.

'What are you doing here?' was all Kell could manage as Gray stopped in front of him.

'I really need to talk to you Justin. Let's say I've got the inside line on a potential scoop for you and your paper. It's a delicate situation and I'm hoping you can help.'

Still on the defensive Kell replied, 'how did you know I'd be here this morning?'

'That's all part of the story Justin. Please just give me half an hour over coffee and I'll explain everything.'

'There's a Costa just around the corner and I'll give you as long as it takes me to drink my Americano.' Kell set off without waiting for a reply.

Gray got the coffee and they sat on stools looking out onto New Cavendish Street.

'First things first,' said Kell. 'How did you know where I would be?' There was nothing friendly in his tone.

'I'll get to that, but it will make more sense if I just tell you the whole story,' replied Gray.

'Ok, go on.'

Gray had thought long and hard about how he would tell a version of the events that had brought him here and whilst he knew that the journalist would have questions, he knew it would be a disaster if he gave away too much at this time.

'I have concerns about the way my firm operates. When I joined them, the business model was already up and running. Once I came on board, I helped with the application for authorisation from the Financial Conduct Authority, but I didn't have sight of the Regulatory Business Plan and I didn't see the full application. The operation is well capitalised, but I have my doubts about the legitimacy of the source of the funds.'

'Who are the beneficial owners?' asked Kell.

'That's just it,' replied Gray. 'I managed to find out that there are a dozen names who all hold about eight per cent, with Bobby Dulac holding the remaining four. These guys must have been checked out by the regulator, but when you look online to see their history, it's all very bland and you quickly reach a dead end.'

Kell interjected, 'That is interesting. I had the same experience when I checked out Robert Dulac. It all seemed very manufactured.'

Seeing he had sparked Kell's interest, Gray asked. 'Would you like another coffee?'

Kell smiled, 'Sure, same again.'

When Gray returned with the drinks, it was Kell who picked up where he'd left off.

'So, what you're suggesting Henry is that the fund is some sort of front, presumably for laundering money?'

'I'm not sure what I'm saying at this stage, but it all just doesn't feel right. The other thing is the FCA is starting to look hard at Life Settlement Funds. A lot of them are struggling to maintain their capital requirements and a number have frozen all withdrawal requests from investors. We, however, have no such problems. We are even buying policies from younger and generally healthy people to supposedly secure a source of long term regulatory capital.'

Kell didn't respond immediately, while he processed what he was hearing. 'That does make some sense, but it's a very confident play. It also suggests that Horizon are planning for the long term, which would be at odds with the money laundering theory as these guys tend not to hang around. Normally they use a couple of sources and then disappear, making it harder for the authorities to trace them.'

Kell continued, 'why don't you anonymously whistle blow to the FCA?'

This was a question Gray had prepared for. 'Any scrutiny from that quarter and an internal leak would immediately be suspected. I'm the new boy in what is a tight knit operation and if what I think is happening is true, then I absolutely do not want to get on the wrong side of these people.'

'Ok, I'm interested,' replied Kell, 'Just one final question. How did you know where I'd be this morning and why didn't you just call me or come into the office?'

Gray responded with his pre-rehearsed answer. 'When you came to see Bobby as part of your article into our sector, he took an immediate dislike to you. I don't think he relished the thought of an investigative journalist digging any dirt on him or the company. A couple of weeks later, I was in his office and saw a folder on his desk with your name on it. He'd just gone out for one of his long lunches so I read what was inside. It wasn't much, just a basic profile of you, background history, education, time you spent in the Met and that you were registered with this Harley Street shrink. It wasn't too difficult to get the details of when your next appointment was, so I thought it best to try and meet you somewhere where it wouldn't be noticed.'

Justin Kell went blank. His eyes stared into space but didn't see anything. He sipped his coffee without knowing what he was doing. It was as though part of him had just shut down.

'Justin, Justin are you ok?' Gray moved to take the coffee cup from the journalist's hand, but before he could reach it, Kell clicked back into reality.

'I find that very concerning. I don't like having my privacy invaded; your boss has crossed a line that should never be crossed.' Kell paused, and stared Gray down as he continued. 'I will look into all this, and I hope for your sake Henry that you have nothing to do with it.'

'I promise you, I don't have any involvement with this Justin. I'm scared of what's going on and hopefully you can see why I came to you with it.'

Kell nodded in acceptance of Gray's explanation. 'I believe you for now. Anything else before I go?'

'There's a guy called Alfio Mignemi who acts like he's Bobby's boss but doesn't hold any position in the firm. I get the impression he's the shareholders attack dog. You probably should check him out as well.'

Kell made a note of the name on his pad, then stood up to leave. 'Let's meet here in a couple of weeks. That should be enough time for me to get a handle on if there's anything in this.' With that Kell left. No handshake, he just walked out of the coffee shop.

As Gray finished his coffee, he patted himself on the back thinking how it couldn't have gone any better. He had the journalist on the hook and given him just enough to ensure he took the bait. He could report back to Dulac that his objective was now work in progress and when the shit finally hit the fan, he would hopefully get the chance to decide whose side he was really on.

Chapter 22

In the two weeks since Amy met Bobby Dulac, she had expectantly waited for the details of where to go for the medical to come through. This was mainly because she was keen for the process to be finalised so she could get her money, but she was also looking forward to meeting the charismatic American again.

She'd asked if the medical could take place in Manchester as it was easier for her to rearrange her diary if required. So when the email arrived confirming this Saturday morning at a private clinic in Wilmslow, she was delighted that it wouldn't interfere with her busy work schedule.

Amy pulled into the spacious car park and was not surprised to see the usual array of top of the range cars that were associated with one of the wealthiest suburbs in the country. She found a parking space and walked across to the entrance and into the reception area. As she approached the reception desk, a familiar American drawl said. 'Good to see you again Amy, how have you been these last couple of weeks?'

Amy turned to see a smiling Bobby Dulac walking towards her with the two kiss greeting completed before she had a chance to say anything.

Quickly regaining her composure, Amy responded. 'Bobby, what on earth are you doing here, you're not involved in the medical are you?' As soon as she said it, she realised how stupid it sounded.

Dulac laughed. 'Not at all. But once you're through, I was hoping you'd have time to grab some lunch.'

Amy had a gym class booked at noon and then a session with her personal trainer which she made a point of never missing. Caught off guard, she replied, 'Of course, that would be lovely.'

'Great, I'll wait for you in my car. It's the Bentley with the driver out front.'

The medical was straight forward and similar to ones Amy had taken before. She'd sent back the questionnaire which asked the standard questions about smoking, drinking and previous health issues and this was quickly ticked off as fine by the doctor. All the usual tests followed, the worst of which for Amy were the blood samples that were taken to test for any hidden nasties. It was all done in forty minutes and she walked out into the spring sunshine to see Dulac pacing around the car park with his phone glued to his ear.

Amy slowed her approach so as not to interrupt and just caught the end of the conversation.

'It's not a risk. I will deal with everything. OK Alfio.' Dulac was clearly irritated by the person on the other end of the call, but as he turned and saw Amy strolling towards him he switched on his big smile with the air of someone who didn't have a care in the world.

He ushered her to the car where the driver was holding open one of the rear doors. She got in as elegantly as she could, glad she had decided to wear trousers and when she was safely inside, Dulac went around to the other side of the car and sat in the back next to her.

'I hope you don't mind my coming up to see you. I've business in Edinburgh on Monday so I thought I'd break the journey to see if you wanted to discuss anything about the policy.'

'I don't mind at all,' replied Amy. 'It's a lovely surprise and so nice of you to think of me. It's a long way from London to Edinburgh, I'd have thought you would have flown?'

'I like the privacy of being driven. I can also get a lot of work done. I've got everything I need in here and there's no security and all the time wasting that goes with getting on a plane these days.' Dulac hesitated as he spoke as though he'd revealed something he shouldn't.

Amy just nodded, having noted the slip but quickly changed the subject. 'Where are we going for lunch?'

'It's a recommendation from a guy I know who lives this way. A small Italian place just outside Alderley Edge called Verde.'

The drive took only fifteen minutes and they made small talk about the weather and the English countryside as they drove. It was just gone midday when they arrived and they were the only people in the place for about half an hour. Amy resisted Dulac's attempts to get her to have a glass of wine. She had to drive back to Manchester and she'd managed to rearrange her personal training for later in the afternoon. She ordered a mineral water and a Caesar salad and Dulac followed suit with the mineral water stating he didn't like to drink alone and chose the beef carpaccio with a kale salad on the side.

'Do you give all your clients this personal attention?' Amy asked almost fluttering her eyelashes at the same time.

'Just the special ones,' replied Dulac. 'You're an attractive lady Amy and you've had a brilliant career. Put those things together and you've got my attention all day long.'

'The career hit a major bump in the road last year. Actually, it was a major car crash. I lost my business, let down a lot of people who were relying on me and I'm just starting to pull myself together.'

For the next hour, Amy recounted every last detail of the rise and fall of AmDesigns. Dulac listened patiently only interrupting to ask the odd question to clarify certain points. They finished their coffee as Amy arrived at the end of her story, 'and here I am today. Hoping to get enough money from my policy to pay the deposit on my new apartment.'

'That's some story Amy. You should be proud of how you've got your career back on track. You thinking of setting up on your own again?'

'Not for the foreseeable future. I gave my word when I got this job that I'd see it through. I'm not going to let anyone else down, that's for sure,' replied Amy.

Dulac smiled, 'All the best of British traits in one lovely lady. That's why I love working here so much, everyone is so honourable and trustworthy.'

Amy laughed. 'I don't think that's always the case. I've had to deal with a lot of shysters in my time.' She gave Dulac a look which almost asked, '*you're not a shyster are you Bobby*?'

They walked out to the car with the driver standing by the open door. When they were in and seat belts on, Dulac switched back to business. 'We'll get the medical by the end of next week. I'll get my PA to email you with our valuation of the policy and at the same time make the arrangements for you to come in and sign the forms, should you still want to proceed. I assume you'll be bringing the accountant with you?'

'Yes, Phil will want to come. He likes to make sure I'm alright. It's kind of sweet really.'

'That's fair enough,' Dulac replied. 'But how about just you and I go out for some dinner after the business is completed?'

'That would be lovely,' replied Amy. 'I can't wait.'

'Great, leave it with me.'

They'd arrived back at the medical centre and it was Dulac who got out of the car to open the door for Amy.

'Thanks for lunch Bobby, it was a nice surprise to see you.'

'My pleasure,' he replied just before gently kissing Amy on the lips.

Dulac's car waited until Amy had left the car park. He knew he shouldn't be getting involved with a client, but she was like no other woman he had ever met. Was he falling in love? He was too old for infatuation but it certainly felt different to anything he'd known before. Would his feelings make it difficult when the time came for the English rose to be "realised"? Probably, but if push came to shove, he'd do it himself. Bobby Dulac could be like that.

Chapter 23

JJ and Sammi sat in her car outside the VA Hall where every Friday evening at 7.30 pm they held the weekly AA meeting. JJ had been rationalising to himself all week that he was managing not to drink on his own so therefore he didn't need the help of exposing his weakness to others. He'd also tried to convince Sammi, but as soon as he raised the subject he knew he'd made a mistake. Sammi wasn't going to force him to go to any particular meeting, but she was adamant that when he was ready, he must make his own decision and start attending.

The digital clock on the dashboard changed to 7.29.

'You OK to go in big guy?' Sammi took hold of his hand as she spoke.

With what felt like the biggest effort of his life, JJ said, 'Sure.' He opened the car door, walked across the street and went into the Hall.

It was a large room which JJ estimated could have held up to three hundred people if the chairs were set in rows in front of the elevated stage. He imagined how back in the day there would have been hundreds of ex-servicemen listening to how their lives were going to get better if only the government would listen. The cheering and the hope. Today, it was that same hope. The hope of a better life; a life free from the addiction of alcohol; a life that had a future.

As JJ walked into the Hall, a guy dressed in a polo shirt and Levi's held out his hand in greeting. 'Welcome to the Friendly Group. Help yourself to coffee and grab a seat.'

JJ sat down on one of the chairs that were arranged in a circle and immediately found an interest in looking intently at his shoes. He'd looked at the different types of meeting with Sammi and understood that this was an open meeting, so anybody, even non-alcoholics could attend. JJ thought that maybe people would think he was just a curious bystander and not someone tainted by the need for a drink.

The meeting commenced with the same guy who had welcomed him, taking his seat in the circle, welcoming everyone to the Friendly Group and then reading the Twelve Steps and Traditions of Alcoholics Anonymous. He then said, 'Who would like to speak first?'

JJ listened as one by one the men and women in the group spoke of what they'd done since the last meeting they attended. In each story, there was a mix of the daily routines of life entwined with their personal battle not to give in to the craving for the drink or drug of their choice. Not everyone spoke. A couple of guys didn't speak at all. One woman didn't share her story but was very supportive when others did, acknowledging their success and being sympathetic to their failures. It was clear that the meeting was about to wind up when the leader asked for a second time if anyone else would like to say anything. JJ realised it was now or never.

'My name is JJ Carmichael and I used to play football.'

JJ shared the headlines of his story, up to the meeting where his contract was terminated and the feeling of emptiness that engulfed him. He hadn't mentioned taking a drink at all.

After a long pause JJ continued.

'I've always liked a drink. After games, I'd have a few beers with the guys and really enjoyed them. At that time I was in control. Strong enough to know when to stop. I had a responsibility to my teammates and the fans. That all changed when I got my injury. You never fully recover from the sort of damage I did to my knee ligaments and alongside the rehab and the pain killers, I started drinking hard. Jim Beam is my poison and I was drinking a lot of it.'

It was too early for JJ to go into the detail of some of his benders, so he fast forwarded to recent events.

'Now I work as a janitor in a local High School and on a Monday morning three weeks ago, one of the staff saved my life.'

By the time he'd finished, there were tears slowly trickling down his cheeks. He ended with. 'That's my story, well some of it. Thanks for listening.'

There immediately followed a chorus of: 'Well done JJ. Keep strong JJ. We're all here for you JJ.' Pats on the back, handshakes and even hugs. The outpouring of love and support was such that it reminded JJ of when they'd won the Play Off final and how the supporters were so happy and ecstatic with what the team had achieved for them.

This was better though. This gave him real hope that he could get his life back on track.

The meeting finally wrapped up and JJ walked out and back across the street to where Sammi was waiting. He got in the car, leaned across and gave his best friend a long hard hug. All he said, all he needed to say was 'Thank you, thank you, thank you'.

At Sammi's instigation, the weekends were developing with an activity-based focus. On Saturdays, they'd started to go and watch the school first team play their matches. As the weeks went by, this developed into JJ helping with warm-up, advising the coach on the plays and running the post-match debrief and analysis. Sundays were all about exercise. JJ and Sammi would go on long bike rides or take a picnic and go walking in the hills. Sammi was also teaching JJ to play tennis.

Physically, JJ was getting back into decent shape. The flab was turning back into muscle, his eyes were clear and sharp and Sammi noticed how he no longer stooped, holding himself upright with a confidence and pride.

Progress on the emotional front was more gradual. He never missed a meeting and slowly he was coming to terms to a life without alcohol. Sometimes little things would trigger a craving, usually when something didn't go as he expected or there was the disappointment of the team losing. But he was getting better at coping when this occurred and Sammi was always there to talk to and lean on if required.

JJ didn't go back to his old apartment. Sammi would drop by once a week to pick up the post and they were coming to the decision that JJ should let it go as the arrangement at Sammi's was working so well.

'Just the usual junk mail this week, but there is an official looking letter as well. It looks like it's come from England,' said Sammi putting the letters on the kitchen table.

JJ picked up the letter, looked at the return address and immediately knew what it was. He opened it, quickly scanned its contents and then sat down and started to shake.

'What's wrong JJ?' Sammi was at his side with her arm around him.

'That!' said JJ pointing to the letter.

Sammi picked it up and read it all from start to finish. 'But this is good news JJ, they'd paid just over $900,000 into your bank for that life policy you had.

'No its not! I don't want the money. I'm happy as I am, as we are. Money just brings problems and I don't want it to spoil anything.' JJ was crying as he spoke.

'Oh my darling JJ, it won't change anything. Here stand up and give me a hug.'

JJ stood up and the next thing he knew Sammi was kissing him. Really kissing him.

When she broke away, she looked him in the eye and said. 'I love you big fella and no amount of money will change that. Just leave it in the bank and forget about it. Let's focus on moving you into my bedroom. What do ya say?'

'I love you too Sammi, I love you so much.'

That evening they talked long and hard about their feelings for each other and if the progression of their relationship could have a negative effect on JJ's progress at the AA meetings.

'We'll have fights and arguments you know JJ, that's natural with any couple. When we do, we can't have you getting black thoughts and heading for a bottle. We're both gonna have to be strong on that, ok?' Sammi had wondered if it was too soon to have shared her feelings with JJ. She knew he was still fragile but she did love him so much.

'I know, Sammi. The guys at the meeting talk a lot about this. Some have lost their wives and husbands because of the guilt and the emotional blackmail. Us alcoholics are good at blaming other people for our faults. I know it won't be easy, but I know what I need to do and I can get there with you by my side.'

Sammi smiled. 'Come on big guy, let's go to bed.'

The next few weeks were the best that JJ could remember. To be in a relationship with so much love and respect was more than he could have ever imagined when he'd been spending his weekends in Declans. When people realised that they were a couple, they were genuinely delighted for them. JJ and Sammi started to get invites to dinner parties and barbeques and everyone respected that not only were they both teetotal but that he was also an alcoholic.

But the one thing that did not change was JJ's attendance at the weekly meetings of the Friendly Club. No matter what invitations they got for a Friday night, Sammi would drive him down to the meetings and wait across the street for him to come out. They'd drive home, have a simple supper and if JJ wanted to talk about anything, Sammi would listen.

Even the Friday at the end of term could not change this routine. The school always held a big barbeque on the sports field for the teachers, kids and their parents and this then continued on to the various teachers' friendship groups carrying on the party back at someone's house. Despite a number of such invitations, JJ and Sammi declined and after meeting a few of the parents they knew at the start of the festivities, they left to go home and then head on to JJ's meeting.

'You sure you don't mind missing out on the fun?' JJ asked as they drove home.

'Just being with you is all the fun I need big guy!' replied Sammi.

They laughed and joked the rest of the way home making plans for what they'd do in the summer vacation.

JJ walked into the Hall, got himself a coffee and started chatting with a few of the guys he'd got close to over the recent weeks. He started to get to the meetings about fifteen minutes before they started as he enjoyed the casual conversations which helped him to get to know everyone a little better.

JJ felt good about life, and whilst he still had the odd craving, he didn't feel the need to share any of his experiences of the past week. The meeting finished up a little earlier than usual and having said his goodbyes, he walked out into the evening sunshine.

He smiled and waved as he crossed the street to where Sammi was waiting in the car.

The men in the van who had been watching this ritual for the past month, pulled out and started accelerating down the street. There was no screeching of tyres or revving of the engine.

Anyone watching would just think it was a van going a bit too quickly in a neighbourhood where such things were normal. The men in the van had been thorough in their preparation. They'd timed how long it took for JJ to walk from the door of the Hall to the car. They'd worked out the speed they needed to hit to ensure they intercepted the target before he reached the car. They'd even had a couple of practice runs. They were approaching JJ from behind; he was blind-sided by their approach. The van was fifty yards from JJ when he heard it. He turned and for that fatal split second he hesitated before realising he needed to move.

Sammi, turned around and saw the van which she'd later describe as being grey or maybe just white and not very clean, closing in on JJ. In her statement, she wasn't sure if the van tried to avoid the love of her life or followed him to ensure they got a hit. Either way it didn't matter. The coroner estimated the van hit JJ at 48 miles per hour. He wasn't killed instantly but he died in the ambulance on the way to the hospital.

The police found discarded bottles and needles in the street near to where the van had been parked. They concluded it was kids who were high and looking for just another cheap thrill.

The police never found the van or got any leads on who was driving. They had numerous other cases that they prioritised over a hit and run.

JJ Carmichael was dead. Just as he had started to find some joy and happiness in his life, JJ Carmichael had been mown down in the street like road kill.

Chapter 24

Since his meeting with Henry Gray, Justin Kell had spent every spare moment looking into the Horizon operation. Initially, this involved just going over and re-checking everything he already had on the firm, but when this drew the same blank, he started to ask around his contacts to see if anyone had heard any rumours or gossip relating to the firm or the mysterious Bobby Dulac.

When this didn't take him any further, Kell switched his attention to the other name that Gray had given him, Alfio Mignemi.

Kell put the name into the news feed search engine that would flag up any article in which the target had been referenced. Based off his previous experiences with anything to do with Horizon, he wasn't holding out much hope, so was pleasantly surprised when the search started to list numerous articles which referenced the Italian. Not being a fan of reading things on his tablet, he printed them out, nineteen in total, and settled back to read them in the hope this would be the breakthrough in the mystery of the Horizon Life Settlement Fund.

Mignemi was born in Beirut in 1959 of an Italian father and a Lebanese mother. He still maintains his family home there in the Lebanon, having gone to Italy with his parents in 1976 after the civil war started.

Educated at the Lebanese University, he then did a Masters in English at Sapienza, the University of Rome, before returning to Beirut when the war was at its height in 1981. He was an active participant in various Muslim Lebanese groups and the alliance with the Palestine Liberation Organisation but seemed to keep himself at arm's length when the Israelis and Syrians started to pick and choose different factions to support.

When the war finished in 1990, Mignemi was associated with various initiatives for the rebuilding of the infrastructure.

His name was linked with a number of shady deals, which was par for the course in a country that was rife with corruption. Organised crime controlled who got which contract and always took their share of the spoils.

Mignemi had various directorships listed, which Kell would check out, although he expected these just to be fronts for whichever crime syndicate he was working for.

When he finished the last article, one thing was clear; Henry Gray was right to be concerned. If Alfio Mignemi was involved with Horizon, then there was definitely something illegal and potentially dangerous going on.

Henry Gray felt it was the calm before the storm. He had his follow up meeting with Kell the next day and the last two weeks had been quiet. Nothing unusual or out of the ordinary had occurred. Dulac had spent a lot of time out of the office, which was not unusual and there had been no sign of Mignemi. There was no suggestion that any of the digging Kell was undoubtedly doing had got back to his masters. In a way this was comforting, but Gray knew it was just delaying the inevitable.

The phone on his desk buzzed indicating it was Dulac's PA.

'Bobby wants to see you in his office.'

'OK thanks, I'm on my way.'

Gray was surprised not to see Mignemi when he walked into Dulac's office, shutting the door behind him.

After the usual pleasantries, Dulac got straight to the point. 'Last week a significant asset was realised. The ex-footballer, $100m coming our way soon. So far the authorities aren't suspecting anything that points to our involvement and we are making sure it stays that way. The life company was notified of the death by the guy's agent, some dude called Sloan, so they've been in touch already, advising that the funds will be transferred as soon as the paperwork is finalised and the police close down their investigation. We are confident that this will be soon, in the next two weeks or so. As soon as the funds come in, I need you to wash it through our internal accounts and transfer $2m to each of these nominee accounts.' He handed Gray a sheet of paper with the details. 'You don't need to worry about how to show this in the accounts and regulatory statements, I'll sort that out. Any questions?'

'Seems straight forward,' replied Gray. 'Have we got anymore big ones lined up?' He hoped this was ideal timing for Dulac to give him a better insight into the scale of the insidious business.

Dulac smiled, mistaking Gray's interest being aligned to a selfish greed. 'I'm personally working on a decent sized case and Alfio is in Europe looking to establish arrangements with various groups we've previously worked with. If things go as planned my English friend, you will soon be a very, very rich man.'

'I'm surprised you're personally involved in a case? Is it in the States?' Gray desperately hoped he sounded casual.

Dulac paused for a moment, before replying, sending Gray's heart rate through the roof.

'Actually, it's here in the UK and I expect to get the papers signed next week. It's a £5m case and let's just say I'm enjoying the chase. Mixing business with a bit of pleasure. Now if there's nothing else, I've got a meeting on the other side of town to get to.'

Back in the dealing room, Gray pondered on what Dulac had said. The firm he worked for had murdered a high profile ex NFL footballer for the $10m his life policy was worth. He personally knew this, so was directly associated with the crime. He was also aware that the killing of innocent people whose policies Horizon bought was the basic premise of the business model. He didn't know the details of who, where and how many but this didn't change the fact that he was also an accessory to these murders. He doubted that anyone would believe that he just managed the assets of the fund and didn't know what was really going on.

His mind drifted back to that Saturday afternoon on a crag just outside Bristol, when he'd been responsible for Mike Jones' death. That had been the start of it. Mignemi and Dulac had targeted him because they somehow knew his deep, dark secret. They'd needed someone like him for the FCA application. An investment manager with no industry profile and no baggage to attract regulatory attention. Basically a patsy they could play.

He was a fool, sucked in by the big money and now he had a choice to make. What would happen if he told Kell all he knew? If he escaped the retribution of Mignemi and Co, would he go to prison? Could he get one of those immunities that always happened in the cop shows on the television or would they lock him up and throw away the key? Christ, this was a mess. It made his concerns re money laundering seem like getting a parking ticket.

But one thing he wasn't going to let happen was for another innocent victim to be killed for the profit of some mafia douche bags.

He opened his Outlook and clicked on Dulac's diary. He scanned his appointments for the following week, noting that a number were hidden behind the private icon. What caught his eye was one that wasn't hidden. A meeting in his office at 5.00 pm a week on Thursday with an Amy Speight. It looked like dinner at the Ivy in the West End followed.

So that's what Dulac had meant when he said he was mixing business with pleasure. Gray didn't think that anything could be as low as what had already happened. But if Amy Speight was an asset to be *realised* by Bobby Dulac, then his boss had just hit an all-time low.

Henry Gray had a decision to make and he had until tomorrow to make it.

Chapter 25

Justin Kell got into the office early. He wanted to check some more details on Mignemi that had come in overnight from a guy he knew who worked for Reuters in the Middle East. It was much of the same thing. Lots of innuendo suggesting links to organised crime but nothing that was sufficient to charge him with anything. Mignemi was on Interpol's watch list but with an "amber flag". This meant the authorities preferred to know where he was but wouldn't hunt him down if they didn't need to. Kell was convinced that Henry Gray wasn't telling him everything he knew. The guy was scared and for some reason regarded Kell as someone who could help him. The more he thought about this the more bizarre it seemed. Gray knew that he suspected him of the murder of Mike Jones and here he was actively seeking him out and asking for help? It simply didn't add up.

The doc had moved Kell's appointment that was scheduled for this morning, but Kell decided not to change the time or meeting place with Gray. It was out of the city, on neutral territory and he wanted to get there early.

He got the Central Line to Oxford Circus and walked up to New Cavendish Street. He was half an hour early and waited towards the Portland Place end of the street where he had a decent view of Costa where he was meeting Gray.

Just before 11.30 Kell started to slowly stroll towards the coffee shop, intently looking at his phone like a tourist fixated on google maps. When he saw Gray go into Costa he stopped and scanned his eyes up and down the street systematically taking in the array of people going about their daily business and discounting them when they were not what he was looking for. Less than sixty seconds later he clocked what he was. He was a man in his late thirties, about six feet tall. Close cropped blonde hair, he was wearing a black bomber type jacket, jeans and a smart pair of trainers. He had a small backpack and was looking at a London guide book. He walked past the coffee shop, crossed the road and sat on a bench that gave him a good line of sight of Costa's window. He got a bottle of water from his back pack and started to read the guide book.

The golden rule was no intervention until you were sure of what you were dealing with, so Kell put his phone away and went to see what Henry Gray had to say.

'I got you an Americano,' said Gray as Kell sat down at the table.

'Thanks Henry, what news have you got for me?'

'I thought you were the one who'd have some news,' replied Gray indignantly, 'you are supposed to be investigating Horizon with the info I gave you.'

'I have managed to make some progress, but I'm sure there's a lot you aren't telling me.'

'Like what?' Replied Gray.

'Like, did you know you were followed here?'

Gray was visibly shaken. 'Followed, by who? Who would want to have me followed?' Gray was trying to keep his voice down but failing miserably.

'Keep quiet!' snapped Kell, 'and listen carefully.'

'I've gone over everything on Horizon again and again and I can't find anything out of the ordinary. From the outside looking in, it looks like any other fund manager. However, I checked out that name you gave me, Alfio Mignemi, and boy is he an interesting character.'

By the time Kell had finished describing in every detail what he'd found on the life of Alfio Mignemi, Henry Gray looked like a broken man.

Kell continued, 'My guess is that your employers have lost their trust in you, Henry. They want to know what you are doing, who you are seeing and how this might threaten their operation, so they can make a decision on whether they should keep you on the payroll.'

Kell described the guy who had followed Henry and where he was sitting over the road from the coffee shop. 'Go and get two more coffees and casually have a look for yourself.'

When he returned with the coffee, Gray sat down with an air of frightened resignation.

'I'm way out of my depth here Justin and I'm terrified of what these people might do. Before I joined, the operation was already up and running. They promote the service of buying life policies people can no longer afford, in blue collar areas across the US. Local advertising campaigns, simple ads in local papers plus word of mouth is all they need to get traction. They buy the policies for a knock down price, pay any premium arrears and get the policy assigned to Horizon. The main targets are impaired lives, so people who have anything between one and five years left.'

Kell interrupted, 'This is common knowledge Henry, you're not telling me anything new here.'

Gray paused before continuing, 'It's simple really. To ensure the regular flow of cash into the fund, if people don't die soon enough, they have them killed. It's made to look like an accident of course. And because these people tend to be in the under classes, nobody takes a lot of notice.'

It was Kell's turn to be stunned into silence. 'You are sure about this Henry?'

'Positive. I don't have access to the client lists. But these would show the trend of the date the policies were purchased, date of death, amount paid to Horizon. I imagine in a court of law this could be seen as circumstantial, but they have upped the ante recently.'

'What do you mean?' Kell was trying to compute everything he was hearing but was struggling to make sense of it.

'Remember I told you they were starting to buy policies off a younger demographic, to supposedly support the long term capitalisation of the fund? Well, there is this ex NFL footballer. A guy called JJ Carmichael. Had a policy for $10m. We bought it about a month ago for $900k. He died in a hit and run last week. I've been given a list of accounts to transfer the money out to when it arrives. But that now seems to be the least of my worries.'

For the next forty minutes, the ex-cop in Kell grilled the fund manager on every aspect of Horizon's operation. They'd been in the coffee shop for so long that the lunchtime rush was at its peak, so Kell bought a couple of sandwiches and checked that they were still being watched. They were.

'So what have you done to make them lose their trust in you?' Kell enquired.

'Bobby doesn't like you. He doesn't want some ex-cop investigative journalist snooping around the operation. So, to ensure I was fully on the team, they instructed me to kill you.'

'What!' cried Kell.

'They basically blackmailed me over Mike Jones' death. I guess they thought if I could do it once I could do it again.'

Justin Kell blanked out. The world around him went quiet, total silence. There was no awareness in any of his conscious senses. To anyone watching him they'd just see a guy eating a sandwich.

'Justin, are you alright?' Gray had seen this happen once before but this time it went on a lot longer. After what seemed like an eternity, but was actually only five minutes, Kell snapped back into reality as though nothing had happened.

'That's why you came to see me. Get close to me. Know my movements. Understand my weaknesses,' Kell's wrath was erupting like Mount Etna on a bad day.

'No, no, no, it's not like that at all. Don't you see. You're the only one who can help me. I can't go to the police, I don't have anyone to turn to except you.' Henry Gray was begging.

Calming down slightly, Kell said. 'Is there anything else you are not telling me?'

'I think their next target is an English woman called Amy Speight. She's about to sell us her policy. Bobby is dealing with it personally. She's coming in next week to sign and then it looks like he's taking her out to dinner afterwards. If there is anybody who doesn't fit the profile of our model it's her. She's young and healthy and high profile.'

'I know that name,' said Kell. 'Self-made business woman but crashed and burned like a lot of people in the financial crisis.'

'That's her. Please Justin we must do something to stop all this.'

'And not get ourselves killed in the process,' mused Kell. He continued, 'OK I need to speak to some people and think out the next step. Let's meet on Friday evening out of the city. How about somewhere near where you live. I doubt they'll follow you home, when they know your routine. Anyway, after seeing us together that's probably told them all they need to know. Let me know the time and place but don't use any work or mobile phone. Even your private one.'

With that Justin Kell got up and left, giving the guy on the bench a little wave as he walked past.

Chapter 26

Back in his office, Justin Kell pulled up everything he could find on Amy Speight. This was a lot easier than finding anything on Dulac and Mignemi as there were hundreds of articles that had been written about her and interviews she'd given on her rise to fame and fortune with AmDesigns. There were also articles that narrated her fall from grace with the liquidation of her group.

As he read, Kell could not help but admire the woman. Growing up in Manchester, she attended local schools and had gone to Manchester University after the statutory year out travelling. She left university in 2001 with a first class degree in Business and Marketing and started work selling advertising space to upmarket magazines. She left to set up her own agency in early 2004 and this quickly grew into a major business doing the promotion, branding and marketing work for a diverse range of companies throughout the UK and Europe.

The view of the financial press was that the group expanded too quickly and with the financial crisis that started in 2008 resulting in a lot of businesses cutting back on their marketing and branding development, the decline of AmDesigns was swift. This was mainly due to Amy Speight deciding to enter voluntary administration with the hope that some of the jobs of her people could be saved.

Now at 31, she had started again as the Brand and Marketing Director of a technology company and articles in the sector's trade press suggested she was already starting to make her mark.

The pictures of her showed an attractive woman of about five feet eight inches tall with shoulder length blonde hair. Her hobbies were noted as keep fit and this was evident from her trim figure. The woman exuded life and for Justin Kell there was no way a piece of scum like Bobby Dulac was going to take it away from her.

When he'd satisfied himself that he had all the information on Amy Speight, Kell turned his attention to the murder of JJ Carmichael that had taken place in a suburb of Chicago. Carmichael had been staying with a friend who was helping him get back on his feet, a teacher called Sammi Renniker. She was waiting for him across the street from the local VA Hall where he attended the Friday evening AA meetings. Since he'd started attending some weeks previously, Carmichael hadn't missed one.

This went someway to confirming Henry Gray's assertion that Carmichael had been murdered. When someone has such a strict routine, its straightforward to plan and execute the easiest way to kill them. The fact that the police could find no trace of the vehicle plus the evidence of drink and drug use left where the van was parked all added up to a professional job.

The thing that struck Kell most about the incident was why the cops had shut the case down so quickly. It all seemed a bit rushed. Surely Mignemi and Co.'s reach didn't stretch as far as the Chicago PD?

Kell picked up his mobile and dialled his old friend and colleague at the Met, Chris Packham.

'Chris, it's Justin. How are you doing?'

'Drowning in the usual pile of paperwork that prevents any proper policing being done these days,' replied Packham. 'How are you Justin, or should I say, what do you want this time? If you love the work so much, maybe you should come back permanently!'

Kell laughed. 'I don't love you or the job that much my friend, but as you ask, there is something I could use your help with.'

Kell had decided not to share the full story with his friend at this stage. One, because he wanted to be sure that he wasn't being duped by Henry Gray in some way, particularly as he was claiming that Mignemi and Dulac wanted him dead. And secondly, if all Gray said was true, then this would be the biggest exposure of an organised crime gang operating through the city of London that the Met would have dealt with for a long, long time. He needed to tread carefully to ensure he stayed at the heart of the investigation and of course, got the story.

'I don't know if you've got any connections in the Chicago PD, but recently there was a murder of an ex NFL footballer, a guy called JJ Carmichael. On the face of it, it looks like a hit and run but I've got reasons to believe it could be more sinister than that. Also, the local police closed down the investigation a little too quickly for my liking.'

'Why on earth are you interested in a murder that took place three thousand miles away! You're unbelievable Justin. What have you got yourself involved in this time?'

'Let's just say there might be a link to a story I'm investigating back here in London. I can't say too much at this stage but it would be helpful if you could get the inside track on the Carmichael murder.'

'Listen Justin. I've got so much on at the moment that it's fourteen hour days, seven days a week. I don't have time to spend on some wild goose chase for a murder in Chicago. Get real!'

'You have to trust me on this Chris. It could be the most important case that you'll ever work on. Please just make a few calls and we can meet next week when I should be able to give you the full picture.' Kell was almost begging, but he knew he had to get Packham on board if he was to have any chance of stopping the Horizon Settlement Fund scam.

'OK, OK, I'll do it. I'll let you know when I've got something.' With that, Packham hung up and Justin Kell sat back in his chair as his mind went completely blank.

When Henry Gray left the Costa on New Cavendish Street, he didn't wave to the athletic looking guy sitting on the bench on the other side of the road. He hailed a cab and headed back to the office. He normally would have got the tube as it would be quicker, but he needed time to think as he was sure he would be greeted by some rather unpleasant questions from Bobby Dulac.

He got out of the lift on the fourth floor at the office in Ely Place and as soon as he walked in the receptionist said. 'Bobby wants to see you in his office and be careful, he's not in a good mood.'

As Gray entered Dulac's office, his heart fell even further when he saw Mignemi there as well.

'Henry, what were you doing meeting with Justin Kell?' Mignemi got straight to the point as usual.

Henry knew there was no point denying his meetings with the journalist so he'd decided to go on the front foot. 'Following your instructions regarding Mr Kell, I studied the dossier that Bobby provided. I decided that the best way to help me complete my task was to attempt to befriend the journalist. This way I could get close to him, understand his movements and lifestyle, which in turn will determine how I complete what you've asked.'

'You expect us to believe that Henry?' Mignemi asked.

'Of course I expect you to believe me. Why would I lie?' Gray sounded genuinely exasperated.

'We think you might be trying to expose our operation in order to save your own skin. Don't we, Robert.'

'We sure do,' drawled the American. 'You see, if you're gonna kill someone, the closer you get to them the more attention you draw to yourself. So that would be a pretty dumb thing to do.'

'Despite what you think, I've never done anything like this before.' Gray was getting angry but it sounded like desperation in his voice. 'You've given me no help with this and I'm supposed to just go out and kill a man and make it look like an accident. You guys are just unreal.'

There was a pause in the conversation and after a minute Mignemi nodded at Dulac.

The American picked up the conversation. 'Ok, calm down Henry. We just have to be sure. We are about to ramp up the operation and we need absolute trust in every one of our employees. You can forget about the journalist. We'll take care of him, so we don't expect you to meet with him again or communicate with him in any way. If you do, then you will be permanently removed from the payroll.'

'Is that clear?' asked Mignemi.

'Crystal. Now I need to get back to work.' With that Henry left the office shutting the door behind him.

'Do you trust him Robert?'

'Yeh, I trust him, but I would like to keep Andrei on his tail just to make sure.' Replied Dulac.

'I hope you are right Robert. As I would hate to lose you as well. Now let's discuss Miss Speight. I'm concerned you may be losing your focus on this one.'

Chapter 27

Henry Gray left a message on Kell's mobile to meet him at seven o'clock that Friday evening at a wine bar called Franco's in the middle of Brentwood. Despite Kell's cautionary words about not using his mobile, he left his personal number so Kell could contact him in case he couldn't make it or was delayed.

Following his discussion with the journalist earlier in the week, Gray understood the importance of getting access to the client lists. He knew which files held the data but all he got was "Access Denied" when he clicked on the relevant drive. He couldn't ask the in house IT guy as this would clearly be reported back to Dulac, so he rationalised to himself that the only way was to use his boss's computer and somehow find his password.

Like most people, Dulac maintained his diary on his iPhone, but he also had a desk diary that Gray had seen him make notes in from time to time. Gray didn't believe that someone like Bobby Dulac would be stupid enough to write down the passwords he used, but you never know.

It was not uncommon for Gray to be the last to leave the office of an evening. With the Dow being five hours behind, he liked to see what the trading activity was like before he shut down for the evening. His boss on the other hand was seldom in the office after 4.30 pm, so when it got to just before six on the day before he was meeting Kell and the office had emptied out, Gray walked down to Dulac's office, settled in behind the desk, switched on the computer and started to go through the desk diary page by page.

When the computer had gone through its start-up routine, he glanced at the screen and was surprised to see under Dulac's user name eight bold full stops in the password box indicating that the password had been saved, so didn't need putting in every time you logged on.

As the screen filled with the usual array of icons, Gray continued to turn the pages of the diary to see if there was anything that looked like it might be a password. There were various notes and names scattered throughout the pages together with the odd phone number but by the time he'd gone through it from start to finish there was nothing that suggested it was a password to the Z drive where the client lists were held. He was just about to give up and call it a night when he noticed a list of random letters on the inside back cover. There were a series of letters which Gray thought matched to the main drives that the company used and against each one a sequence of characters that looked exactly like what he was looking for.

He went to the Z drive and double clicked to open it and was greeted with the password box. He carefully entered the mix of upper and lower case letters and the #3 at the end. He hit the return key, but instead of the various files he expected to appear, *Password Incorrect. You have two more attempts.* Gray just stared at the message as the realisation of what he'd done hit him like a sledgehammer. Would this failed attempt to log in be flagged somewhere? The answer was probably, yes, to the IT guys. Would they think it suspicious and report it to Dulac? Gray thought on the balance of probability that they wouldn't. He thought about his own passwords and how he changed them when he got the three-monthly reminders. He simply used the same word and changed the numeral on the end. Would a guy like Bobby Dulac adopt the same approach? He concluded that he could have one more attempt, but if that was wrong then he'd have to leave it. If Dulac got locked out of the Z drive, then all eyes would be looking at him, going straight to jail without passing Go.

He needed those client lists but reckoned he had a few more days to get them. He decided he'd see what Kell thought before trying again next week. He shut down the computer, closed the diary, carefully putting it back exactly in its place and headed home.

Justin Kell had decided to trust Henry Gray. The guy was frightened of what he'd gotten himself into and was clutching on to Kell like a drowning man holding a life belt in a stormy sea. Whatever happened with what was going on in Horizon, Kell now knew that Henry Gray did have a hand in the death of Mike Jones. When the dust eventually settled, Henry Gray's career would be over and justice would be done. Before then, Kell had to ensure that he kept him alive. With this in mind, he decided he'd follow the fund manager for the couple of days before they met on Friday evening. He doubted that Gray was in collusion with anyone but thought it likely that men like Dulac and Mignemi would want to know who Gray was seeing and exactly what he was doing.

On the day before their meeting, Kell waited in the MacDonald's outside Liverpool Street station. He got a coffee and sat in the window waiting for Gray to appear. He knew he usually walked up to his office instead of getting the Central Line to Chancery Lane, and as it was a warm and sunny morning the odds were he'd see his quarry walking passed him any minute.

Sure enough, five minutes later Gray appeared, slightly stooped due to the backpack he always carried, walking with his usual purpose. Kell waited, carefully scanning the stream of commuters who were spewing out of the station concourse heading for places of work where they would be trapped for the next eight hours or so. He only had to wait about thirty seconds before he saw a familiar looking athletically framed guy with short cropped blonde hair heading in the same direction as Gray.

Kell didn't need to follow them. He knew where they were going but this did cause a problem for the meeting they had planned for tomorrow. He knew from experience that it was virtually impossible to lose a tail on foot, so they would need to be a bit more inventive.

Back at his office, Kell picked up his phone and dialled the main number for Horizon.

'Horizon Group, Hayley speaking how can I help you?'

'Could you put me through to Henry Gray please?'

'Who shall I say is calling?'

'Arnie Smith from Morningstar.'

Seconds later it was Gray's voice on the line.

'Henry Gray speaking, how can I help you?'

Kell had decided that if Henry's calls where being monitored, he doubted that they would be religiously listened to each day. Calls through the main switchboard may be logged but the majority of fund managers use Morningstar and he hoped his approach would not attract any suspicion.

'Henry, its Justin. Don't say anything, just listen until I've finished. The guy who followed you when we met the other day, is still on your tail. I imagine your employers are keen to keep you in their sights. This means we have to be careful when we meet tomorrow. I suggest that when you get off the train in Brentwood you go for a drink. In the meantime, I'll go straight to your house and you can get your wife to let me in. I doubt he'll maintain surveillance on the house all night, but once I'm inside we can keep out of sight. Do you understand?'

Gray was trying to take in everything he was hearing. All he could come out with was.

'Are you sure?'

'I'm certain Henry. I will be on the same train as you out of Liverpool Street tomorrow, so will let you know if our friend has taken the evening off. Just let your wife know that I'll be calling round. Ok?'

'OK Justin, see you tomorrow.'

The 17.49 from Liverpool Street to Brentwood was packed as normal on a Friday evening. Kell watched Blondie as he had nicknamed him, get onto the train in the carriage behind the one where Gray had boarded. Kell just managed to squeeze himself onto the back of the train and when it arrived in Brentwood, waited until the last minute before getting off.

He spotted Henry walking up the steps to exit the station, with his tail about twenty yards behind him. He waited five minutes until the next train pulled in and joined the masses to leave the station where he jumped into a cab to take him to Gray's. It was close enough to walk, but he wanted to get there quickly and reduce the chance of being noticed.

When the cab pulled up outside a large Georgian styled detached house in a quiet cul-de-sac, Kell realised he was in the wrong job. Henry Gray was clearly being paid very well by his employers. He rang the doorbell and was greeted by Carol Gray who was clearly on her way out. Full make up, bling everywhere, a short skirt and clutching a designer handbag, she greeted him with.

'You must be Justin. Make yourself at home. I'm off out with the girls. I thought that was my taxi until you got out of it. Oh, here it is, see you later.' And with that she was gone.

Kell did a quick recce of the house and settled himself upstairs in a small study come office, which had a window looking out over the back garden.

Half an hour later he heard the front door open as Henry got home. When the door was closed Kell called out. 'I'm upstairs in the study Henry.'

'Ok, I'll be right there.'

Gray entered the study looking tired and drawn. 'This is a living nightmare, Justin,' he said as he sat in the only chair in the room apart from the one behind the desk where Kell had established himself.

'One way or another, it'll be over soon. Just hang in there Henry.' Kell tried to sound as reassuring as possible. 'Did you manage to get the client lists?'

Gray recounted his attempt to access the Z drive and his thoughts on the potential password. 'When you told me I was being followed I thought it was because they knew I tried to access the client lists! I hardly slept at all last night. Man, I'm so scared.'

Kell kept to the business in hand. 'I agree with you about the password. It could be that it now ends with #4 or even 5. Or maybe it's just a reminder that you need to spell out 3. Mmm, you are right though; you've got one more or three more chances depending on how you look at it and then I think it will be time to make yourself scarce.'

'What progress have you made? Please tell me you've got something on them.' Gray sounded like a broken man.

'I've got a contact in the Met looking into the Carmichael murder.' Kell paused before continuing.

'You mentioned that Dulac is signing up Amy Speight next week and then taking her out to dinner?'

'Yes, to The Ivy in the West End. Why?'

'Here's my plan.' Kell's mind was whirring as everything began to fall into place.

'I will also be at The Ivy next Thursday. I'll arrange to meet my contact there and he can update me on what he's found out about the Carmichael case. I'll make sure Dulac sees us and that it's clear my dinner guest is a cop. This will hopefully make Dulac realise that they can't take out Miss Speight as it would just be too risky. At the same time, you will have another go at accessing those client lists. Subject to that and depending on what my contact can come up with on the Carmichael case, it will hopefully be enough for the police to get a warrant to search Horizon's offices.'

'What about me?' asked Gray.

'Whether or not you get the client lists, you and your wife will need to disappear for a while. I'll see if you can go to a police safe house, but if not, you'll need to avoid Blondie. Your testimony will be key to convicting these bastards and come Friday morning, they will want to silence you permanently.'

'Testify, you didn't say anything about testifying!' Gray was almost sobbing as he spoke.

'It's the only way Henry, otherwise these guys will just move on and destroy countless more lives. So, what do you say, are you in?'

Reluctantly Gray replied. 'Yes, I'm in.'

'Ok, on Thursday let me know either way if you get the client lists. Suggest you post them to my office and take photos on your phone as well. Then get out of town without being followed.'

Kell left through the back garden, which backed onto fields, and then looped around back to the front of the house. As he thought, Blondie had now picked up a car which was parked at the end of the cul-de-sac.

As he headed back to the station, Kell hoped that Henry Gray was up to this and didn't go and do something completely stupid.

Chapter 28

The Metropolitan Police have links with all the major police forces throughout the US. This is achieved through a number of Liaison Centres across the States that collate and deal with requests for information on crimes committed on their soil. It was a surprisingly efficient arrangement with copies of case files being sent through a secure line within seventy two hours.

Detective Inspector Chris Packham had just finished reading the circumstances surrounding and the investigation of JJ Carmichael's murder and could see why his journalist friend had concerns. Why he was interested in such a case was another matter that Packham intended to find out.

The Investigating Officer was called Lund, a Detective of the same rank as Packham who was noted as the contact point if any further information was required. They had agreed that Lund would give Packham a call at 18.00 BST to discuss those things that wouldn't have made the case file.

Just after 6.00 pm, Packham's phone rang.

'DI Chris Packham. How can I help you?'

'Chris, it's Troy Lund from the Chicago PD. You've an interest in our ex footballer case.'

'Thanks for ringing Troy. Yes, there may be a link to something that's brewing over here, so I'm interested in any background and your instincts on the case. I've read the case file the Liaison team sent through and it seems the case was closed down very quickly.'

'That's the smuck of the DA we're dealing with over here. No sooner had our initial findings gone in, the DA's office determined that it was NWP.' Lund's feeling about the decision were clear from his tone.

'NWP?' asked Packham.

'Sorry Chris, "Not Worth Proceeding". We get a lot of them simply because we don't have the resources and despite what you read, serious crime is on the way up over here.'

'Did you think it was a straight forward hit and run?' enquired Packham.

'No, I did not. It had all the features of a professional hit, made to look like an accident. In some ways it was too perfect.'

'What do you mean too perfect?'

'They tried to make it look like kids had been drinking and snorting coke. Forensics confirmed traces of the drug amongst the bottles of liquor that had been discarded where the van was parked. You know what was wrong with this, Chris?'

'If you're going to snort coke, you don't do it in a van parked on a side street in downtown Chicago?' answered Packham.

'Got it in one, buddy. It just doesn't add up. The fact that we couldn't find any trace of the van also suggests a professional operation. But as for motive, well that's where we hit a brick wall. OK the guy was famous. He'd been to the Super Bowl a few years back. But he's a school janitor, a recovering alcoholic. Who'd want to kill him?'

'What about Sammi Renniker?' She was at the scene at the time,' Packham asked.

'Her and JJ had just hooked up together. She was helping him with his alcohol problem and they were living at her place. She'd taken him to the meeting, same as usual and was waiting outside for him. The van came from her blindside so she didn't see anything. Poor woman is devastated.'

'What about his finances?' Packham had reached the last question on his list.

'A couple of months ago he'd sold a life insurance policy and got about $900 grand. But he owed virtually all of this to the IRS, so he was basically broke when he died.' Lund paused before continuing. 'I can understand why the DA decided it was NWP, but man the decision came back quickly. Just 48 hours when it normally takes them at least four weeks.'

'Thanks Troy, that's been helpful. Just one more question, who did Carmichael sell his life policy to?'

'A firm called the Horizon Group,' came the reply. Lund continued, 'what's the London Met's interest in this case then?'

Packham replied, 'I think you've just answered your own question. Thanks again Troy and I'll keep you posted if anything develops over here.'

Packham smiled as he ended the call, *so that's why you're interested my financial journalist friend.* He opened up Google and searched for Horizon Group.

The next day Packham rang Kell to arrange to meet so they could update each other on what they knew about the JJ Carmichael murder and the link to Horizon. Packham had not found out a whole lot about Horizon's activities in the UK other than they were a fund manager who operated in the Life Settlement sector and seemed to be doing quite well. He had no doubt that his friend would be able to fill in the blanks.

'Justin, what can you tell me about the Horizon Group then?' The policeman's opening question got straight to the heart of the matter.

'Very good, Chris, you're not just a thick plod after all.'

'Very funny. Now you've got my interest, when can we meet so you can explain what's going on?'

'You are going to book a table at The Ivy on Thursday for 7.30 pm. You are going to use your police powers of persuasion to ensure we are sitting in direct sight of the table that's been booked by a guy called Bobby Dulac.'

Packham interrupted, 'The CEO of the Horizon Settlement Fund.'

'Very good Chris, I told you you're not just a thick plod! We'll meet for a drink at seven o'clock and I'll fill you in on everything I've got, but I imagine you are putting two and two together and getting an even number.'

'OK, but you're paying. I can't afford to eat in places like The Ivy on a DI's salary.

'It will be my pleasure,' replied Kell. 'See you Thursday.'

They arranged to meet in The Whit Hart in Covent Garden, just a two minute walk from the restaurant. Kell was waiting outside in the warm late spring sunshine when Packham arrived. He handed the DI a pint of lager.

'Cheers, boy do I need this,' said Packham, before gulping half of his drink down. 'Ah, that's better. Now, please tell me why we are having dinner at The Ivy?'

Kell told the story from the beginning. The death of Mike Jones, Gray moving to Horizon, how Horizon was bucking the trend in the sector and delivering good returns, the likely link to organised crime via Mignemi and his belief that they had been murdering people to get a prompt return on their investment.

Packham didn't say anything until his friend had finished. 'Interesting. But there's a lot of circumstantial evidence.'

'I know,' replied Kell. 'But hopefully Gray will get access to their client lists this evening and surely that will be enough for you to get a search warrant.'

'Maybe, maybe not,' mused the DI. 'Let's go back a few steps. You're saying that they targeted Gray because they suspected he was responsible for the death of Mike Jones and this would give them some leverage over him if he discovered what was going on.'

'Yes and when this is all over, Henry Gray needs to be held accountable.' Kell was not going to let that one go come what may.

Packham picked up where he had left off. 'The involvement of Mignemi and the death of Carmichael are sure to get the interest of the CPS but I agree that the client lists are essential if we are going to blow this thing open. What is the plan for the restaurant?'

'Quite simple really. I just want Dulac to see me with you and realise you're a cop. Then just wait and see what he does. It will hopefully stop their plans with Amy Speight and might just make him do something really stupid. If I hear from Gray that he's got the client lists, then we could push him a bit further to see what happens.'

'OK, better get going it's nearly quarter to eight already,' said Packham.

Getting the right table had been straight forward. Packham had spoken to the manager in his capacity as a police officer on a surveillance operation and been assured that they would be sitting just across from Dulac. He didn't know how to make himself look like a DI from the Met as his friend had requested, so he just wore a white casual shirt and black trousers.

As they were being shown to their table, Kell spotted Dulac and his dinner guest, who looked far more beautiful than her pictures in the journalist's opinion. He made no attempt to get eye contact, knowing that it wouldn't take long for the American to clock him. That was if he ever took his eyes off Amy.

The waiter brought the menus and as he started perusing the ridiculously expensive starters, Kell caught Dulac staring intently in his direction. He jokingly raised his menu to hide his face. 'He's seen us and he doesn't look happy,' said Kell.

Packham had asked the restaurant to make a real fuss when serving them; to treat them like they were celebrities. Kell ordered an expensive bottle of wine to go with their mineral waters and the sommelier made a loud point of announcing what an excellent choice it was.

The meal continued without incident. When Kell and Packham had started on their main courses, the waiter came over to ask them if everything was to their satisfaction.

The name tag on his shirt was Marco. 'The gentleman on the table opposite has also enquired who the tall guy is,' he said topping up their wine. 'I told him I thought you were a very important policeman.' Marco looked at Packham and smiled.

Packham grinned, 'thanks, I could do with a promotion!'

'I think that's hook, line and sinker,' said Kell. 'Time I paid a visit to the gents.'

'Why do you keep looking at those men on the table over there Bobby. You've gone very quiet. Are you OK?' Amy asked, sounding genuinely concerned.

'I think I recognise one of them who is a reporter. I get very nervous when I'm near a reporter.' He laughed trying to make a joke of it. 'Excuse me. I need to go to the washroom.'

Kell was washing his hands as Dulac entered the toilets.

'What's a guy like you doing in a place like this?' asked Dulac trying to keep the contempt out of his voice.

'Bobby, what a coincidence seeing you here. How are things going at Horizon? I'll be publishing my article next week. It will include a biography of your boss Alfio Mignemi,' Kell sounded all bonhomie.

'Be careful Mr Reporter, you don't know who you are messing with.' Dulac's tone made it very clear this was a threat.

'Ah but that's just it, I know exactly who I'm dealing with. Now if you'll excuse me I must get back to my guest. You don't want to keep The Met waiting, do you?' Kell brushed passed Dulac as he returned to his table.

131

'What did our American friend have to say then?' enquired Packham.

'He's not very happy and actually threatened me,' Kell smiled. 'I just hope Gray has got those client lists, otherwise things will get messy very, very, quickly.'

When Dulac got back to his table, he signalled to the waiter for the bill, and left with a confused looking Amy Speight.

At that precise moment Kell's phone pinged, indicating he had a text message.

It just said two words. *Got them.*

'Bingo, Gray has come through. Now it's over to you Chris and I suggest you move quickly.'

Chapter 29

'What on earth is the matter with you Henry? The last few nights you've done nothing but toss and turn, I'm surprised you've got any sleep at all. I certainly haven't.' Carol Gray looked at her bleary eyed husband across the kitchen table and was worried about what she saw. Her husband had not been eating at all recently. Drinking far too much, even on week nights and clearly wasn't sleeping. He looked gaunt and was on edge all the time.

'You should go and see the doctor Henry, you look terrible. What will people at work think if you turn up looking like that,' Carol gestured in her husband's direction as she said it.

Gray didn't bother answering. He knew there was no point.

His wife continued the usual continuous stream of verbal diarrhoea. 'It's Thursday remember. So I'll be at my Pilates class when you get in and then I'm going for a bite to eat with the girls. There is a portion of lasagne in the fridge which you can microwave.'

As he trudged out of the house to walk to the station, Henry Gray wondered if he would be going home that evening. Although he knew he was being followed, at no time during the past week had he seen any evidence of his tail. He just knew that the blonde guy was there somewhere, watching his every move. If this wasn't enough to keep him awake at night, all he could think about were the various permutations that could make up Dulac's password. Whenever he thought he'd logically whittled it down to his final three, another potential sequence would randomly pop into his head. He'd written them all down in his notebook.

#4. #Three. #three. #THREE. Then maybe the # wasn't a part of the password, just a prompt to remind Dulac that there was a number at the end. It could even be just the number of the month. They were in June now, so it could be 6, or Six or SIX or six.

And so his mind kept twisting and turning but never finding its way out of the maze.

Anyway, today was the day he had to decide and whether he got it right or wrong, he understood that Kell's advice to lie low until matters sorted themselves out was sensible, but he had no idea how to go about something that sounded so straight forward. He reckoned that he had the weekend to decide. It was unlikely that they'd be on to him as quickly as the next day. So when he got home on Friday, he'd surprise Carol with a last minute break to somewhere far away.

Despite the routine of the office and the daily tasks that needed to be completed, the day dragged slowly for Henry Gray. But unlike a child on Christmas Eve who for once can't wait to get to bed so when they next wake up it'll be Christmas, it wasn't excited anticipation that filled him but stone cold fear.

Once it finally got to five o'clock, the office started to empty. Gray walked out to the water fountain to get a drink and glancing across to the reception area noticed a rather attractive woman sitting with a middle aged man. So, the famous Amy Speight thought Gray. He could see what the attraction was to Dulac. The guy next to her was probably some sort of adviser or accountant, doubtless in attendance to make sure his client didn't get ripped off.

Gray walked back to the dealing room to continue his nervous wait, when his phone rang.

It was Dulac's PA. 'Bobby wants to see you in his office.'

Bloody marvellous. Now he had to put on his serious professional face for Dulac's latest quarry.

Dulac beamed as Henry Gray walked into his office. 'Henry, this is Amy Speight and her accountant Phil Jones. Amy, Phil meet Henry, our fund manager.' They shook hands and Gray sat in the only available seat at the side of Dulac's desk.

'Amy is a potential client and Phil has a few questions for you Henry, before they put pen to paper.'

'Sure, what would you like to know,' said Gray in his best professional voice.

'I understand the basic tenets of a life settlement fund, but why is Horizon thriving when there is so much speculation across the industry that these are toxic, high risk investments. Even the FCA are starting to have concerns.' Phil Jones's tone was earnest and he clearly wasn't going to take any of the standard promotional sound bites at face value.

Gray could feel Dulac's eyes boring into him as he answered.

'In simple terms, we take a much longer view than our competitors. The mortality rates we use indicate a return of 15% to 20% over a seven to ten year period. We are also very well capitalised. We established a considerable bank of assets before we opened the fund to investors. In the model used by others in the sector, they use the funds of their investors to purchase the assets, in this case life policies. This is just like any other fund, but with the added risk that you don't know when people are going to die. Some of our competitors got their mortality assumptions wrong, or people are just managing to live longer. Our capital base is such that we don't have to rely on the policies paying out to meet any withdrawal requests from investors.'

Jones interrupted, 'What do you do then? Why does a fund like yours need to employ an expensive fund manager?'

'Firstly, it's a regulatory requirement. Whatever asset classes a fund holds it needs to have an authorised fund manager in situ, fully vetted and approved by the FCA. Secondly, our net position is such that we are able to invest a proportion of what are regarded as liquid assets into the usual stocks, bonds, gilts and cash to maximise the return for our investors.' As he was speaking on familiar territory, Gray started to relax and almost enjoy himself.

'OK, but why are you purchasing policies from people like Amy?' Jones clearly still needed convincing.

Gray continued, 'Just to be clear, it is not as though we are going out and buying up every policy we can get hold of. Far from it. We are very selective in this area and in fact we are only looking for a very small number of such policies, to secure a specific figure as per our business model. That figure of course is confidential. I would also add that policies that fit our criteria are hard to find.'

Dulac stepped in, 'And of course you approached us. Now if you've no more questions for Henry, I'm sure he's got lots to be getting back to.'

'Thanks Henry, that's helped my understanding a lot.' Jones finally seemed to be satisfied.

Duly dismissed, Gray went back to his desk in the dealing room and waited.

Half an hour later, Dulac put his head around the door and said, 'All done and dusted. I'll send the assignment off to the life company tomorrow and we'll transfer the funds to Amy early next week. You did good in there Henry, very impressive. Just remember to keep your focus.'

'Thanks Bobby, and don't worry, I will.'

It was gone seven thirty when Henry was satisfied that everyone had gone and would not be coming back for any reason. He also wanted to be sure that Dulac would be ensconced at The Ivy before he embarked on what was probably going to be his "coup de grace".

In Dulac's office he started up the computer and clicked on the Z drive. As before, Dulac's user name was pre populated and the cursor was blinking at the start of the password box.

His hands were shaking as he entered his first attempt. The start of the password as noted in Dulac's diary was unimaginably random. StAtSiDe and then the # symbol. Gray carefully typed these in and then entered his first choice StAtSiDe#three.

The response immediately came back. *Incorrect Password. You have two more attempts.*

'Shit, shit, shit!' Gray said to no one but himself.

He steadied himself and then tried again; StAtSiDe#Three.

Incorrect Password. You have one more attempt

'Bollocks!' Gray was now sweating profusely.

'In for a penny,' he said to the room and started typing StAtSiDe#THr…

'Now, now Henry, what are you doing in Robert's office that is causing you so much anxiety.'

Mignemi stood at the door with a familiar athletic looking blonde guy standing just behind him.

'I was just, just … looking for something.' Henry Gray did not sound convincing at all.

'Shut down the computer and tell me exactly what you are doing Henry. Oh, and if I don't believe you, Andrei here will take over the questioning.' Mignemi sat down in the chair on the opposite side of the desk as he spoke.

Gray started to babble. 'I didn't know what to do. The reporter is threatening to accuse me of the murder of Mike Jones if I didn't help him. He's been to my house and threatened my wife. I'm just so scared Alfio, I don't know what I'm doing.'

Mignemi looked at Blondie. 'Has Kell been to his house?'

A strong eastern European accent answered, 'No sir.'

'It was the other Friday.' Gray was pleading now. 'Kell was following me and he saw you. He made me go for a drink and went straight to my house before my wife went out. He threatened her and waited for me. Then started saying all these things about the evidence he had against me on Mike Jones.'

'Is this possible Andrei?' Mignemi's tone had a slightly harder edge.

'Anything is possible. I wasn't aware I was being followed.' Blondie did not sound too concerned at this failure on his part.

'We'll talk about this later,' said Mignemi.

Mignemi turned back to Gray. 'What were you doing on Robert's computer.'

'Kell wants our clients list. I think he's onto what we are doing and thinks they will help him. He's waiting for me to confirm if I've got them or not.'

Gray avoided telling Mignemi that at that moment Kell was in The Ivy winding up Dulac. An oversight he would later regret.

'Text him that you've got them. Then we are going to have a serious talk Henry. A very serious talk.'

Chapter 30

'Before I take this upstairs, I want to review those client lists and the associated evidence. So let's meet with this Gray character tomorrow and we'll take it from there.' Chris Packham was ninety per cent convinced that there was a serious crime being perpetrated but he didn't want it blowing up in his face if the evidence wasn't credible.

Kell and Packham were so engrossed in their conversation that they didn't notice the figure approaching their table.

'You don't mind if I join you?' said Amy Speight pulling out a chair and seating herself opposite Justin Kell.

'Not at all,' replied Kell. 'Can I get you a drink?' Kell just stared at the beauty opposite him.

'Nothing for me thanks, but I would like some introductions. I'm Amy Speight.' She held out her hand first to Kell and then Packham who shook it politely.

'I'm Justin Kell, a financial reporter. I work for the Fund Management Journal. And this is Detective Inspector Chris Packham from the Metropolitan Police. I thought we'd just seen you leave with Bobby Dulac?'

'Yes, but as soon as we got outside he took a call and had to go to an urgent meeting. He called me a cab, but I thought I'd like to meet the people who seem to have got under his skin.'

It was Packham who interjected, 'Miss Speight, please be assured that I am not here on official police business. Justin is an old friend and colleague and we are just catching up over a quiet dinner. I'm not aware that we got under your friend's skin as you put it, but if we did and it spoiled your evening then I apologise.'

It was Kell's turn to chip in, 'Some months ago, I did write an article on Mr Dulac's firm, the Horizon Settlement Fund with the help of one of his colleagues, Henry Gray, but that was just part of a series I was doing on boutique fund houses. I think it showed Horizon in a positive light.'

'I met Henry Gray earlier this afternoon when I was concluding some business at Horizon's offices. He's their fund manager isn't he?'

'Indeed he is.' Kell decided to provide as little detail as possible at this stage.

Amy Speight had a keen sixth sense and knew there was something going on here that they weren't telling her. Both men were very charming and professional sounding but it was the reporter that intrigued her. She decided to get straight to the point.

'When I was at Horizon's offices earlier, I completed the transaction to sell them a life policy. They are paying me a shade under £250,000. Should I be concerned about getting the money?'

Kell and Packham exchanged glances, that did not go unnoticed by Amy Speight. It was Kell who responded. 'I have no doubt whatsoever that you'll receive the proceeds of the sale. Horizon are a well-capitalised business. Why don't I send you the article I wrote on them? It will tell you everything you need to know. Now if you'll excuse us we are just about to pay our bill and leave.' Kell opened his wallet and pulled out a business card. 'Feel free to call me anytime if you want to discuss anything.' He smiled as he handed her his card.

She looked at it carefully before putting it in her purse and getting out one of her own and handing it to Kell. 'Likewise,' was all she said before standing up and leaving the restaurant.

'She's one confident lady,' said Packham.

'Indeed she is,' mused Kell, turning her card over and over in his fingers. 'But back to business. I'm sure she's safe for the time being; I doubt they'll act too quickly, especially as Dulac knows we've seen them together. I'll make contact with Henry and arrange a meeting for the three of us to go over those lists. With a bit of luck, we can have this wrapped up in a couple of weeks tops.'

'Don't get too carried away my friend. You know as well as I do that it's all about the evidence. Unless we get something concrete, this case won't get to first base, let alone get wrapped up.'

On the other side of the city, Henry Gary was sitting nervously in his boss's chair as Mignemi finished his call with Dulac. 'Meet us at the boat as soon as you can and make sure you are not followed.' It was the first time that Gray had ever heard the mysterious Italian sound worried.

'Andrei, bring the car around, we are going down to the dock.'

As they drove south east across the city towards the river, Gray was desperately thinking of ways he could get out of this complete clusterfuck he'd got himself involved with. He realised that it was just about staying alive. Getting away from these maniacs who go round killing people and finding some place to hide away until they were locked up. How to achieve this was a different matter, for all he knew he could be dead within the hour.

The dock turned out to be St. Katherine's Dock, just by Tower Bridge. The boat, Sophie's Dream, a Broom 50. An impressive fifty feet of boat with four berths, two toilets and sea going capability. When they were settled in the main cabin, Mignemi and Gray sat opposite each other at a modest sized table, with Andrei standing by the door to the main deck. There was another door at the rear of the cabin which Gray assumed went further into the bowels of the boat.

Thirty minutes later, Dulac arrived, looking decidedly unhappy.

'Are you sure you weren't followed Robert?' Mignemi had regained his calm authoritative tone on the drive from the office.

'Of course I wasn't followed, but I did have company at the restaurant.' The look Dulac gave Gray was pure cold, hard menace.

'I assume you are referring to our reporter friend,' enquired Mignemi.

'And a fucking cop! I think they're on to us Alfio. I think we need to go straight to Plan B.'

'Mmmn, that does change things somewhat.' Mignemi turned his attention to Gray. 'What do you know about this policeman Henry?

'Nothing, I swear. Honestly nothing.' Henry Gray was babbling to save his life. 'We know he was in the Met before he became a reporter. It was in that file you gave me on him, Bobby. He must be following you or something.'

'I think I'd have noticed if I was being followed. Maybe the woman has something to do with it?' Dulac was calming down as he considered the possibilities.

'I thought I'd warned you about getting involved with a client Robert. We'll talk about that later. For now we need to consider our next move. My associates have a lot of money tied up in this operation and we are not just going to walk away.'

All eyes were on Mignemi. It was clear no one else was to say anything until he'd decided what they were going to do.

'I can find out if the Police are looking into us with any conviction. They are usually paralysed by the CPS who won't give the go ahead for anything that is less than certain to lead to a prosecution. This leaves the reporter, who must be removed. Henry, Mr Kell believes that you have the client lists which he regards as an important piece of evidence. What arrangement do you have to hand these over to him?'

'I was supposed to post them to his office and keep an electronic copy as well.'

'I see. You will contact Mr Kell and arrange to meet him at one of the bars on the marina. Tell him he must come alone. No police. We will arrange to follow him to ensure that he complies. Arrange the meeting for Tuesday next week. From tomorrow and over the weekend you will start to transfer all our funds to designated accounts that I will provide. When you meet Kell on Tuesday, you will bring him here. We will kill him and dispose of his body out at sea. Actually, you can kill him. This will be your last chance to save your own skin. Otherwise, you will join Kell at the bottom of the North Sea.'

Mignemi turned his attention to Dulac. 'How quickly will the assignment of the Speight policy take?'

Dulac replied, 'I can make a few calls and get it completed within the week.'

'Good. Then we'll arrange for Miss Speight to have an untimely accident. Once we get her funds through, we'll exit the country and leave the Police chasing their tales.'

'Andrei, take Henry home and keep a very close watch on him.'

'Henry, I will see you in the office in the morning when I will give you the account details for the transfer. Now go with

Andrei before I change my mind and put you out of your misery here and now.'

Gray followed his minder up the stairs and off the boat. Dulac went to follow before Mignemi said, 'Not you Robert. We are going to have that chat I mentioned.'

Chapter 31

As soon as Gray and Blondie left Sophie's Dream, Mignemi unlatched one of the cabinets above the table and pulled out a bottle of whiskey.

'Let's have a drink and think everything through. We've come too far to make any stupid mistakes at this stage.' Mignemi gave Dulac a knowing look.

Immediately on the defensive, Dulac replied, 'The broad won't give us any problems. I'll cut all contact with her and by the end of next week she'll be dead.'

'What is your proposal for the hit, Robert?'

'She's a very keen runner. She's training to do some half marathon up north in September, so every spare minute she's either training in the gym or running on the roads in the Manchester countryside. I propose we use the cocktail of non-steroidal and anti-inflammatory drugs to induce overheating and salt depletion. This will produce a viral infection of the brain membrane and the ensuing meningitis will kill her.'

'How will you get the drugs into her system?' Mignemi was familiar with the outcome but not the process of this particular method of poisoning.

'We have a fine powder that dissolves instantly in water and is even more effective in isotonic drinks. It should be quite straight forward for one of our associates to slip it into her drink when she's running at the gym. When the symptoms start, our agent will go to her aid and ensure she consumes more of the drug until there is no coming back for Amy Speight. A hot environment like a gym will speed up the process. She'll probably die in the ambulance before even reaching the hospital. I've already got our guy, I should say girl, attending Amy's gym, so it's just the opportunity we need. I've pretty much got her routine pinned down, so you can see Alfio, that it was just purely business with me and Miss Speight.'

Mignemi smiled, 'Impressive Robert, very impressive. Now with regards to Tuesday, I propose that we are both here when Gray arrives with Mr Kell. Once I'm satisfied that all is in order, I will leave the oversight of Kell's demise to you. I am flying back to Beirut on Tuesday evening to meet with our masters and hopefully convince them that this operation has been a success. The £5m from the Speight policy will help, but the laundering operation now totals nearly £300m and the life policy income over £200m so I think I can persuade them to keep us both alive.'

'What do I do with Gray and when do I get out?' Dulac's tone had a nervous edge.

'Dispose of Gray at sea with the reporter. Ensure Andrei follows the usual discipline. All fingers removed and dissolved in acid before disposal and no dental records. The remains of the bodies will eventually wash up somewhere, but identification will be impossible. You can fly to Beirut once the Speight money has been processed. With Henry out of the way, you will have to do this personally, so the sooner the better. Now I suggest we go and get some sleep, we have a busy time ahead of us.'

Justin Kell was in his office before 7.00 am on Friday morning. He hadn't slept much at all following the events of Thursday evening as all kind of thoughts and consequences consumed his mind. Somehow, the whole shit storm just didn't feel right. Why hadn't Henry been in touch to let him know where he was? What should he do about Amy? She was in genuine danger but how could he tell her that Dulac was a murderer without looking stupid? And then there was the police. Chris was adamant that he wouldn't get officially involved until there was serious evidence on the table. He was interested in the Mignemi angle, but he still thought this could all be the product of the over active mind of a journalist looking for the big story.

His reverie was broken by the ringing of his mobile phone. 'Justin Kell, how can I help you?'

'Justin, it's Henry.'

'Where are you Henry, you had me worried for a while when I didn't hear from you last night.'

'Don't worry, everything went really smoothly. I've got most of the client lists, but as I was finishing downloading them, I noticed another folder which had a load more data in it. I didn't want to risk staying any longer, so I'm going to get the rest on Monday evening.'

'Monday evening!' Kell sounded incredulous.

'Calm down Justin, it's all right. Dulac and Mignemi are flying to the States on Monday afternoon, coming back on the red eye overnight on Wednesday. So I'll have plenty of time to get the remaining client details.'

Gray was actually quite proud of this deception, which in his mind sounded authentic.

'So where are you, at work?' Kell was processing what he was hearing and it wasn't making him feel any more comfortable.

'Yes, at work. I don't know if I'm still being followed but I thought it best just to act normal until we've got everything.'

'Ok, I understand. You're probably right. I'm just a little jumpy after bumping into your boss at the restaurant last night. He was quite agitated when he left.'

'I'll let you know if he says anything about it today. That's if he comes in of course. Anyway, let's meet Tuesday evening after work. There's a pub at St. Katherine's Dock, called The Dickens Inn, I'll see you there at, say 6.30?'

'Ok, Henry, that's fine, see you then.' Kell ended the call with a growing sense of discomfort. Tuesday seemed a long time away which meant there would be no progress with the police until the end of next week at the earliest.

Amy Speight was intrigued by the events of the previous evening. Bobby Dulac hadn't been in touch since abandoning her outside the restaurant and then there was the rather tasty reporter with his policeman friend. Was it a coincidence that they were in the restaurant at exactly the same time as her and Bobby?

Her meetings on Friday morning finished at lunchtime and she spent her time on the train back to Manchester finding out everything she could about Justin Kell. Google was the usual god-send, providing links to numerous articles on Kell's career. That he was previously an officer at The Met didn't surprise her, although the lack of detail on his career was interesting. His time as a journalist was well documented. He'd won various awards in the financial sector for his work and was clearly highly regarded. In his late thirties, he was nearer her age than Bobby, not that she really believed there was any future with the American. But as well as some missing details of his previous career, there was no connection between Kell and Dulac. Uppermost in her thought was getting the £250k for her policy; so long as that came through next week, she'd probably forget about the mysterious goings on with the Horizon Life Settlement Fund.

As she got off the train at Piccadilly, her mobile rang. She didn't recognise the number so let it go to voice mail. Once she had ensconced herself in the cab which would take her back to the office she listened to the message. *'Hi Amy, this is Justin Kell. We met last night at The Ivy. Amy, this will sound stupid but I really need to speak to you. Please give me a call back and I'll explain. Thanks.'*

Mainly due to her concern that she was about be ripped off by Bobby Dulac, she decided to return Kell's call once she was back at her office.

'Hello Justin, this is Amy Speight. You left me a rather intriguing message earlier.'

Kell had debated all morning whether or not to contact Amy. He came to the conclusion that as he believed her life was in danger it was better to look stupid rather than risk anything happening to her.

'Yes, thanks for returning my call Amy. I thought I should explain what was going on between me and Dulac last night. It's complicated, so I was wondering if you were back down in London next week so I can explain face to face.' Kell was trying not to sound too desperate.

'Ah, so you want a date. Is that it,' Amy teased.

'No it's not like that. It is important though.'

'That's disappointing, a date with the ace reporter would be rather nice.'

Kell was getting flustered. 'Er yes. I didn't mean that I don't want a date, I would, but this is important Amy.' Kell felt like a teenager begging for the attention of the best looking girl in the class.

'I'm only teasing Justin, but I'm not in London next week. Can it wait till the following week. I'm there from Monday to Wednesday then?

'No, it could be too late by then.'

The line went quiet as neither one spoke.

Amy broke the silence. 'Why don't you come up here and see me then? I usually come into the office on Saturday morning before going to the gym. Why not meet me here at say 11.00?'

'Yes, yes that will be fine. I've got the details on your card. I'll check the train times and aim to get there for 11.00.'

Amy smiled. 'Wonderful, see you then and I'm intrigued about what you are going to tell me. Bye Justin.' And with that, she hung up thinking men are just like London buses, there isn't one for ages and then two come along at once.

This one however, was more interesting.

Chapter 32

Was she flirting with me? Kell replayed the conversation he'd just had with Amy Speight. Maybe she was, maybe she wasn't but at least he'd get the chance to talk to her about what was going on at Horizon and his concerns for her safety.

It was late in the afternoon and he couldn't concentrate on the article he was drafting on volatility in the European markets. All he could think about was what he was going to say to Amy without sounding like a complete fantasist.

He agreed to keep Packham up to speed with when they could see the client data together with any other developments so he dialled his mobile hoping he wouldn't get his voicemail.

'Chris, its Justin. How it's going?'

Packham sounded his usual phlegmatic self. 'Same shit, different day. What have you got for me?'

'Gray's accessed some of the files, but he believes the bulk of them are in another folder. He's getting these on Monday. Dulac and Mignemi are flying to the States on Monday afternoon for a short visit. I'm meeting him at St. Katherine's Dock on Tuesday evening.'

'Good, sounds like progress. He didn't go into hiding then?'

'No Chris, he didn't. And that's just it. Something just doesn't feel right. He's gone from being a rabbit trapped in the headlights to sounding ultra-calm and composed.'

'Do you want me to come with you on Tuesday? If he's setting you up, you'll need some back up.'

'Thanks Chris, but he was insistent I meet him alone. But I wouldn't mind you having my back. We're meeting at The Dickens Inn at 6.30.'

'Consider it done,' said Packham. 'Bye the way, I've got interest from upstairs on our friend Mignemi. Special Branch have him on their watch list over possible connections to the financing of arms trafficking and money laundering, so I've got a genuine reason to pick him up should I bump into him.'

'Well that's a start,' replied Kell. 'The other thing to tell you is I'm going up to Manchester to see Amy Speight tomorrow. I feel I've got to let her know the danger she could be in.'

'Wow, you're a fast mover Justin. Staying the night are you?' Packham laughed.

'It's not like that,' Kell could feel himself blushing.

'I believe you,' replied the detective not attempting to hide the sarcasm. 'Just remember though, there is no official police investigation into all this. So it would be embarrassing if she contacted the local Plod and they started to ask questions.'

'Understood. But I assume I'm OK to give her your number if she wants to check me out?' Kell was relieved that his friend hadn't put the blocks on his trip North.

'Sure, no problem. Now I've got a ton of paperwork to get through, so unless there are any more developments, I'll give you a call on Tuesday ahead of you meeting Gray.'

'Thanks Chris, really appreciate your help with this.'

Kell headed out of the office wondering whether he should pack an overnight bag for his excursion up north.

He had booked on the 8.00 am train out of Euston which would get into Manchester Piccadilly just after 10.00. The first class carriage was quiet and he passed the journey drinking the endless supply of very average coffee and preparing what he was going to say to Amy. In the end, he decided to simply tell her everything he knew, going all the way back to the Mike Jones climbing accident up to their meeting in the restaurant.

It was a beautiful early summer morning in Manchester as the train pulled into Piccadilly just five minutes late. There wasn't a queue at the taxi rank and the roads were nothing like the chaos of London; so at 10.45, the cab pulled into the car park of Amy's office.

The door was locked and no one answered when he buzzed through to reception. He rang Amy's mobile and she answered immediately. 'Hi Justin, I'll be right down to let you in.'

Amy appeared a minute later, dressed in what was clearly her gym gear. A tight fitting gym top and leggings with a running vest over the top. She held out her hand in welcome. 'Good to see you Justin. Thanks for coming all this way just to see me. It

149

must be something very important to get you out of the big city on a Saturday.'

Kell followed his host through the reception area to the lifts.

'My office is on the top floor. Being out of the city, there are decent views across to the Peak District.'

Speight's office was a decent size with the standard desk and meeting table, but also a small settee and an easy chair on either side of a coffee table.

'Would you like coffee or tea?'

'Just water thanks, I'm full of what Virgin trains call coffee. I think it might have put me off for life.'

Speight laughed, 'Tell me about it. When I do that run, I take my own flask.' She opened a bottle of still water and poured two glasses, putting them on the coffee table.

'Now, what is this all about Justin?'

'It's probably easiest to go back to the very beginning. There was fund manager called Mike Jones who died in a climbing accident…'

It took Kell an hour and a half to tell the full story. Everything, no omissions including his appointments at Harley Street, but not going into the details. He concluded, '…and finally we had our chat at The Ivy on Thursday night and here I am.'

Amy had not interrupted him once. She listened intently to every word not wanting to break the flow of the story.

When it was clear the narrator had finished Amy broke her silence, 'That's some story Justin. Very scary if it's true and clearly you believe that I am next on the list?'

Kell was politely forceful. 'It is all true Amy and yes I think you need to be very careful. These guys will go to great lengths to achieve what they want.'

'OK, I've got lots of questions Justin, but first I've got to go for my run. I'm doing the Wilmslow half marathon in September and I'm struggling to get the miles in. Darya my training partner is meeting me outside at 12.30 and we plan to do ten miles. It should take about an hour and a quarter, so I suggest you wait here. When I get back, I'll have a shower and we can go for lunch. We can talk more then.'

'Sounds like a plan. Can you give me your Wi-Fi code so I can log in and get some work done?'

Amy went over to her desk and picked up a plastic card which had all the details for the guest Wi-Fi. She handed it to Kell, 'Now don't go anywhere, I haven't finished with you yet.'

Kell took the time Amy was on her run to finish his article on volatility in the European markets. He felt a great weight had been lifted off his shoulders. Just the relating of the events that had brought him here today had been cathartic.

Just over ninety minutes later Amy walked into her office, showered and changed into a pair of tight fitting blue jeans and a short sleeved white blouse. She looked completely invigorated after her run.

'Come on, let's go and get some lunch. There's a country pub about twenty minutes from here that does great food.'

The locks on the office where all electronic, Amy set the alarm and they walked to the only car in the car park, a white Audi A3 with a personal plate, AMY 1. The conversation was casual on the drive to their lunch venue.

'I assume you must do a lot of running if you've entered for a half marathon?' Kell enquired.

'I used to do a lot but when I had the business it was difficult to find the time. Usually hotel gyms either first thing in the morning or last thing at night. Just the times when it's the last thing you feel like doing. It's a bit easier now with this job and the gym I use is close to where I live. Darya, that's my training buddy, is great. She only joined the gym a couple of weeks ago but we immediately hit it off. She is running the half marathon as well and is really pushing me to put the miles in.'

The cogs were turning in Kell's brain. 'Darya, isn't that a Polish name?' He asked.

'It depends how you spell it.' Amy replied. 'Darya is originally from Russia, but she's lived over here for years.'

The conversation was interrupted as they pulled into the car park of The Fox and Hounds. They found a table by the window looking out onto open fields and the hills in the distance.

'What would you like to drink?' asked Kell.

'Just a mineral water, please and I'll have the open chicken sandwich on granary,' replied Amy.

Kell perused the menu and ordered the steak pie and a pint of Light Brigade. He brought the drinks back to the table and Amy started with her questions.

'What time train are you booked on?'

'I've got an open ticket, so any time really. I've no plans for the rest of the day.' Kell had decided not to pack an overnight bag.

'What did you do in the police and what made you leave to become a journalist?' Amy got straight to the point.

Kell was careful with his response. He'd been through situations like this with Bhati and he had his stock answers that wouldn't bring on any anxiety. 'I progressed through the ranks and got involved in investigating everything from shop lifting to murders. Towards the end, I did a couple of undercover assignments, but I can't talk about the details. I've always enjoyed writing so I left to become a journalist in 2004.

'What made you think that the climbing accident was suspicious?'

'Call it a policeman's instinct. But when I started to read the details of the case, it just didn't add up. It's hard to cock up the safety checks before you start a climb and Gray was the leader of the group. Mike Jones might have been impulsive but I believe Gray knew his harness wasn't secured properly and when he saw his opportunity, he let Jones fall to his death. I interviewed Gray a few months after the event and when I mentioned that fateful day, he blew a gasket and stormed off.'

Amy was following a logical sequence in her thought process. 'How did he get the job at Horizon?'

'It's my belief that Dulac and Mignemi specifically targeted him. The accident was widely reported and somehow they knew that Gray was involved. They appointed him knowing that they'd have something on him if he got wind of their full operation.'

'So why haven't the police intervened yet? It all sounds plausible if not somewhat extreme for this country.'

'At this point, the evidence is all circumstantial. On its own even the footballer's death in the States is just co-incidental. We need to prove there is a pattern, so there is "just cause". We hope the client lists I mentioned will provide this.'

'So cutting to the chase, you think that now I've sold my policy to them, that I'm next on their hit list?' Amy did not sound too concerned but Kell could tell she understood the gravity of the situation.

'Yes,' he replied. 'Which is why I came all this way to warn you to be careful.'

'And there was me thinking it was because you liked me.' Amy grinned as she replied.

Kell got a bit flustered but surprised himself when he replied, 'I do like you Amy and I don't want anything bad to happen to you.'

Being a gentleman, Kell paid the bill and when Amy suggested a stroll in the summer sunshine, he gladly agreed.

It was his turn to ask the questions, so Kell asked her about her career and for the next hour, as they walked down the country lanes of Cheshire, she told him everything about the rise and fall of AmDesigns.

It was three thirty by the time they got back to the pub car park. Kell was disappointed when Amy said, 'I'll run you back to Piccadilly if you like?'

All he could come up with was, 'Sure, thanks.'

As they approached the station Amy said, 'Let's have dinner a week on Monday when I'm next in London. My treat as you paid for such an expensive lunch.'

'I'd like that. I'd like that very much,' replied Kell. 'Have you got a busy week coming up?'

'The same as usual but I'm really enjoying the challenge. The hard part will be the training. 'Darya's insisting we run every day to get the miles in our legs. A mix of the treadmill at the gym and out pounding the streets. I'll probably be a physical wreck at the end of it all.'

She stopped the car on a double yellow line a couple of streets from the station.

She leaned across and kissed him on the lips. 'See you soon Justin. I'm really looking forward to seeing you again.'

'Me too,' was all he could reply. 'Me too.' As he shut the door he said, 'And Amy, remember what I said, please, please be extra vigilant.'

With that, he shut the door, waved her off and walked to the station with a spring in his step.

Chapter 33

Gray was surprised at the scale and complexity of the money moving operation that Mignemi had given him. Hundreds and hundreds of transactions for a maximum amount of £9,999 with some being as small as £1000. He could tell from the IBANs that all were overseas but not the specifics of the country. The total must have amounted to tens of millions of pounds. Gray had worked all weekend on transferring out the money with Mignemi dropping in periodically to check on progress and provide the details of more accounts for the money to go to.

Monday morning was no different as Mignemi was waiting in the dealing room for Gray to arrive.

'Good morning Henry, I trust you had an enjoyable weekend?'

'Fine thanks, Alfio. But as you know I was here for most of it and no doubt Andrei has already briefed you on how I just went home and stayed indoors.'

Mignemi smiled, 'We need to increase the scale of the transfers. You will see that additional monies have been placed into the dealing account. This is to be moved in amounts of £1m to these accounts.'

Gray scanned the paper that Mignemi handed him. There was roughly a couple of dozen account numbers listed.

'These are the last transactions until we receive the Speight money. We expect this to be by the end of the month. Once this has been completed, your employment here will cease. You will receive a modest bonus for your efforts, but I recommend you make plans to leave the country. The scale of what we've achieved here will certainly attract attention and will come with a substantial prison sentence should you be apprehended. The price of your silence to the authorities is your life. Should it emerge you have disclosed the personnel and methods of this operation, you will be killed. Do you understand?'

Gray was so used to such threats that he answered by rote, 'Yes Alfio, I understand.'

'You are meeting Kell at 6.30 pm tomorrow. Make sure you are on the boat by 7.00 pm. We need to conclude the business quickly to ensure we can make the evening tide. I will come back this afternoon to confirm everything here has been completed.'

With that, Mignemi left.

Henry Gray was functioning on auto pilot. He could not comprehend how his life had come to this. He often thought back to the day at CAM when John Harding had told him his bonus was £4,000. The dismay, the feeling of being completely undervalued, the dread of having to tell Carol and wondering if his life was always going be one continuous disappointment. Now he wished so much that he could go back to all that. Those familiar feelings of inadequacy and insecurity would be joyous compared to the paralysing fear he now felt.

He had started to look into opening bank accounts in Switzerland and the UAE, but the process took time. He didn't really believe that he could just leave the country, never to return and lead a meaningful life. Tomorrow, they wanted him to kill Justin Kell. As with most things in his life, he doubted he'd be able to do it. What would happen then? However it played out, he had no doubt he was a dead man.

For Justin Kell the wait until the meeting with Gray on Tuesday evening was increasing his anxiety levels. He hadn't felt so ill at ease since he was at the Met. By the time Chris Packham rang him on Tuesday afternoon, his stress levels were hitting new heights.

'Hi Justin, how's it going?'

'The waiting around doing nothing is killing me Chris. It's all a bit of a struggle really.'

Packham immediately got the strain his friend was under, 'Calm down Justin. It's only a couple of hours till the action starts and this will all be over. I'll be in place with my DS at the dock and I've got a plain clothes to follow you from the office. Any sign of trouble and we'll be right there. OK?'

'That's good to know. Thanks Chris.'

For the last few days, Gray had started to feel decidedly unwell. He had a nagging headache all the time and was constantly thirsty. When he got home, instead of relaxing with a couple of beers all he did was drink copious amounts of water.

When Justin Kell walked into the Dickens Inn just before 6.30, Gray was sitting at a table near the bar with a glass of water in front of him.

'Christ Henry, you look terrible. Is everything OK?' Kell's concern was genuine.

'I feel like shit Justin. I'm putting it down to the stress of what's going on. If it wasn't for our meeting, I doubt I'd have come into work today.'

'What are your symptoms?'

'Constant headache, I feel very dehydrated all the time and I've started to develop a rash.'

'Give me the client lists and we'll get you to the hospital.' Despite Gray looking like he was at death's door, Justin Kell had his priorities.

'Come on then,' said Gray. 'I've hidden them on the boat.'

'Which boat?' Kell was immediately on the alert.

'It's OK, it's docked just out there,' said Gray, pointing in the general direction of the dock. 'I only discovered the other week that the company has this boat, Sophie's Dream. Bobby uses it sometimes to take clients out. He thinks it impresses them and ensures that no one can overhear what they're saying. I hid the client data on there. Even if they knew I had it, it would be the last place anyone would look. With Bobby and Alfio flying off today, it's a perfect place for us to go through it.'

Gray got up and headed out of the bar with Kell following. It sounded reasonable and Kell was reassured that the police were watching. He hadn't picked up that he was being followed when he left the office, so the guy must be good.

There was always an impressive array of boats in St. Katherine's dock and the one Gray was heading for was no exception. Kell didn't know a thing about boats but Sophie's Dream would certainly make an impression on anyone.

They stepped onto the deck and Gray trudged over to the saloon style doors that led down to the main cabin.

'It's easier if you go down backwards,' said Gray as he started the descent. Kell followed, carefully placing his feet on

156

each step. When he got to the bottom he turned around and his mind went blank when he saw the welcoming committee.

'Good evening, Mr Kell. We are so glad you could make it,' said Mignemi.

Kell stood there stock still. You wouldn't know he was breathing without getting very close. No one said anything.

'Mr Kell, please take a seat over here.' Mignemi gestured to a lone chair set slightly away from the table.

Justin Kell did not move. His blank out was total.

'This has happened before when he was with me,' said Gray. 'It's like he shuts down for a few minutes. He will snap out of it, we just need to be patient.' Gray slumped onto the bench at the back of the table.

'What's up Henry, you don't look too good?' said Dulac.

'I feel terrible Bobby. Banging headache and no energy. Can I have a drink of water please?'

Dulac opened a cupboard and tossed a bottle of water to Gray. 'Same brand as you've been drinking in the office the last couple of days. It's our own special mix with special qualities. Guaranteed to make you feel like you wished you were dead.'

Gray remembered the new brand of water that appeared in the fridge at the office. It was flavoured and tasted quite nice.

'You are chronically dehydrated Henry. If you kept drinking this stuff, you'll be dead in 24 hours. I guess you've been drinking lots of water at home, otherwise you'd be heading for the morgue.' Dulac smiled as he spoke.

'Very good Robert. I'm impressed. And this is the same formula that Miss Speight is drinking in large quantities as she works out at the gym?'

'Sure is. In that environment, it will work real quick. And the beauty is that she'll keep drinking more and more the thirstier she gets.'

They all turned as Justin Kell coughed and started rubbing his face as though he was wiping sleep out of his eyes.

'Excellent, Mr Kell is back in the room, now we can get down to business.' Mignemi gestured to the lone chair again and Justin Kell went and sat down.

Chapter 34

When Justin Kell had a blank out he was usually fully aware of what was going on around him. He could hear what people said and could see what they were doing within a narrow field of vision. The condition he had just meant that he couldn't respond to anything until the synapses in his brain rebooted and he started to function normally again.

It all clicked into place very quickly. Amy and her new friend at the gym who by chance was also planning to run the Wilmslow half marathon. The drink that would completely debilitate her and then kill her. The lack of suspicious circumstances that would mean the proceeds of the life policy would be paid out on the presentation of the death certificate. He needed to get off the boat quickly to warn her and then get himself up to Manchester to protect her until all this was over.

Mignemi broke his reverie. 'You have become a problem to us Mr Kell and I don't like leaving any loose ends when we conclude business. Your meddling into our affairs, with the assistance of our colleague Henry here, means that you have left us with no choice other than to silence you both permanently.'

Gray moaned and laid down on the bench.

'I will leave you in the capable hands of Robert and Andrei. The captain of this boat, Phillipe, is also armed so please don't try anything stupid. Robert, let me know when this business is concluded. Now if you'll excuse me.' Mignemi went to leave.

Kell knew he had to do something if he had any chance of getting out of this mess. 'I was followed here by the officers from the Met. They are waiting for you on the dock.'

Mignemi exchanged a look with Dulac but did not change his demeanour. 'I will instruct Phillippe to set sail on my way out. Andrei, prepare to cast off. I don't have a problem talking to

Mr Packham about the beautiful weather we are having for the time of year.'

As Mignemi left, Dulac pulled out a gun and pointed it directly at Kell. 'Just stay very still, Mr Reporter. You don't want to die before your time now, do you?'

His DS had joined Packham on the public walkway that led from the bars and restaurants down to the moorings. 'I didn't expect a boat to be involved. This changes everything,' said Packham.

At that moment a figure appeared on deck, got off the boat and was heading straight for the policeman. The boat had cast off its mooring ropes and was slowly backing out of its berth.

'That's Mignemi,' said the DS. 'Shall we arrest him?'

Packham responded, 'We can't arrest him but we can pull him in for questioning. We also need to follow that boat. Get onto the River Police and give them details and call for uniform back up and a car so we can take Mignemi in.'

As Mignemi approached, Packham pulled his warrant card. 'Alfio Mignemi?'

'Detective Inspector Packham, how can I help you?' Mignemi oozed confidence and self-belief.

'Please can you accompany us to the station. We'd like to ask you some questions.'

'I have a plane to catch, so unless you are arresting me, we'll have to have our chat some other time.' Mignemi went to push pass the two officers.

Packham knew he couldn't let his quarry go. 'Alfio Mignemi I'm arresting you on suspicion of the involvement in the death of John Joseph Carmichael in Chicago on 20th May 2010. You do not have to say anything but it may harm your defence if you do not mention when questioned something which you later rely on in court. Anything you do or say may be given in evidence.'

'You are making a very big mistake Detective Inspector Packham, a very big mistake.'

To Packham's relief, an unmarked police car screeched to a stop on the road above the dock and two plain clothes officers jumped out and raced down the walkway to where they were standing. As Mignemi was led away Packham saw Sophie's Dream pulling out into the river, with no sign of the River Police anywhere. He rang his Superintendent and briefed him on the arrest, which was technically sound, but with no solid evidence, Mignemi's lawyer would have him out by the morning. The only way they could hold him longer would be if Special Branch had anything solid to re-arrest him on.

The DS's phone rang. 'The River Police will be here in five minutes. Do you want me to go with them?'

It was protocol that as the arresting officer, he should go back to the station to book the arrestee into custody. But his friend was on that boat and there was only one thing that was going to happen if he didn't stop them. 'No, I'll go. You go and book Mignemi in. The Super will let you know if Special Branch want to get involved.'

A couple of minutes later, the River Police Boat pulled into the dock. Packham jumped on board and they headed off in pursuit of Sophie's Dream.

Once they were out of the dock, Sophie's Dream kept to the regulation eights knots per hour as she headed down river towards the estuary and the North Sea. Blondie had hurriedly tied Kell to the chair he was sitting in and Dulac hauled Gray from the foetal position he'd adopted on the bench.

'I'm surprised you didn't realise which side your bread was buttered on Henry. You thought you could double cross us but there was no way that was going to happen,' drawled Dulac. 'Now get to your feet, so we can get you ready for your little swim.'

Gray just moaned as Dulac dragged him to his feet and guided him to a door at the rear of the main cabin.

'Andrei, you take care of Henry, I'm going to have a little chat with our reporter friend here to find out exactly what he knows about our operation.'

As Blondie dragged Gray out of the main cabin, Dulac put his gun on the table and sat down on the bench facing Kell.

'What are you going to do to him?' Asked Kell. Gray managed to stop in the doorway and turn towards his boss.

'Same as is going to happen to you. Andrei will inject him with a fatal dose of our cocktail. He'll be dead in about a minute. His fingers and thumbs will be cut off and his teeth removed. We'll weight him down in a body bag and when we're out of the estuary, dump him overboard. It will be a few weeks before he washes up somewhere, but no one will be able to identify him.

160

But enough of that. Tell me what you know and I might just make sure you're dead before we cut your fingers off and smash your teeth out.'

Kell stared at Dulac and smiled. 'The police know I'm here. They followed me to the dock and right now I imagine that your boss is in a cell awaiting questioning and very shortly the River Police will be alongside to take you into custody.'

Kell noticed a flicker of doubt cross Dulac's face. He picked the intercom off its cradle and buzzed the main deck. 'How long until we are out of the estuary?'

'Another twenty minutes, we're restricted to eights knots per hour.'

'Any signs we're being followed?'

'Negative.'

'Ok, let me know if anything changes and be prepared to hit the gas if anything comes on the sonar.'

'Roger that.'

Dulac cradled the intercom, checked his phone and saw he had a strong signal. He called Mignemi's number but it just rang and rang.

'Ok, now cut the crap and tell me what you think you know about us?'

'I know you're a scumbag who doesn't know how to treat a lady.' Kell smiled.

Dulac leapt to feet, picked up the gun and smashed it across Kell's face.

Kell heard a sharp crack as his cheek bone smashed and blood spurted from his nose and lips. He managed to turn his head and look his assailant in the eye. Dulac's eyes were bulging as he raised the gun for another blow.

This time Kell saw stars as the gun smashed into his head. He was desperately trying to hold onto consciousness when he heard the ship's intercom buzz which coincided with a massive jolt as the boat rocketed forward.

Dulac picked up the intercom and listened, before asking, 'Can we outrun them?'

Whatever the answer was, Dulac didn't like it. He put the intercom down as Andrei burst into the room.

Dulac didn't give him time to ask the obvious question. 'It's the River Police. Phillipe is not sure we can outrun them, so let's prepare for a battle. What's Gray's status?'

'He's dead. I injected him a few minutes ago. I was just about to start on the fingers…'

'Throw him over the side. They'll probably stop to pick him up, which will give us time to get away.'

Blondie disappeared out of one door and Dulac the other, leaving Kell alone desperately trying to untie himself.

Henry Gray was aware of being dragged from the cabin. He was also aware that in all probability, his miserable life was about to end. The main words going through his mind in the last few days were "if only". *If only he hadn't gone on the climbing trip; If only he hadn't let Mike Jones fall to his death; If only he'd turned down the job at Horizon and stayed at CAM; If only he wasn't such a greedy bastard; If only, if only if only…*

He watched Blondie preparing the hypodermic with its lethal cocktail and decided he didn't care if he lived or died. He was sorry for all the bad things he'd done but he was a miserable excuse for a human being and deserved to pay with his life. He didn't resist as Dulac's henchman pulled up his sleeve and injected the deadly poison into his arm. As he drifted into oblivion all he could think was, 'I'm sorry Mike, so very sorry.'

Chapter 35

Packham briefed the officers on the Police launch as they headed out of St. Katherine's Dock. 'There is a strong probability that the targets on the boat are armed. So I recommend you get authority to release some fire power from the armoury. There are also two civilians on board; Henry Gray and Justin Kell. Justin used to be one of us. Left the force five years ago and is now a journalist. He's a good guy and a friend of mine. The boat is called Sophie's Dream, she's got a good start on us so let's get a move on.'

John Dean, the skipper and commanding officer of the RIB, took this in and radioed back to base for authorisation to open the armoury. 'The speed limit on this part of the river is eight knots, so we should catch up to them quickly. Everyone to their stations. Chris, I'm happy for you to CO the operation, just tell me where you want the boat to go. If they start shooting, it's going to be difficult to board them so I'll radio the Tilbury station for back up.'

'How fast can this thing go?' asked Packham.

'Top speed is around 50 knots. This makes us one the fastest things on the river, so catching up won't be a problem,' replied Dean.

They sped past Canary Wharf in no time. The river had the usual miasma of different crafts going through their daily rituals. Dean and Packham were on the bridge taking it all in, with Charlie Smith who was piloting the vessel. Dean turned away from the sonar screen he was scrutinising, 'There's a vessel at 700m that has just significantly picked up its speed. Now running at 35 knots. I guess that's them.'

The tension mounted as they closed on their prey.

'When we are in hailing distance, order them to slow down and stop and prepare to be boarded,' said Packham. 'If they don't respond, take their waters and see if we can push them towards shore.'

'What's that they're dumping over the side?' Dean had binoculars trained on the boat. 'Christ, it looks like a body. Charlie, move to intercept. We need to pick it up.' Jones slowed the RIB and turned towards where the body was floating. They pulled up as close as they could and pulled it to the side of the boat with the extendable poles that looked like they had a lasso on the end. They pulled the body onto the boat and Dean checked for a pulse.

'Nothing there. Get the defibrillator and get back on the trail of that boat.'

Packham steadied himself against the railing on the side of the boat and looked on as John Dean put the paddles against the chest of Henry Gray. 'That's Henry Gray. He was the guy Justin was meeting. Christ John, we've got to catch them, Justin could be next.' He had to shout to make himself heard.

Dean put the paddles down and checked again for a sign of life. 'Nothing doing. This guy's dead. I'll radio a code red, which will raise this as a terrorist incident. That should get everyone's attention,' he shouted.

Charlie Jones yelled to anyone who was listening. 'Looks like they've topped out at 42 knots. Got them at 840 meters out. We're going to need help to stop them quickly. Interception time 19 minutes.'

'Counter terrorism have launched a helicopter; their ETA is similar to ours and our Tilbury boat is on its way. These guys won't be getting away,' there was no hint of doubt in Dean's tone.

Kell wondered what was happening as the boat dramatically increased its speed. He was frantically trying to loosen the knots that secured him to the chair. As with the table and bench, the chair was bolted to the floor of the cabin but it did swivel a full three hundred and sixty degrees. He continued to try and work his wrists through the rope and was just beginning to feel a bit of give when the G force of the boat's acceleration jolted him back in the chair and sent it spinning in the opposite direction. A split second later Kell gathered himself and noticed that the sudden movement had somehow slackened the grip of the rope on his wrists. He started to work himself free when Dulac burst into the room with Blondie just behind him.

Dulac was boiling with rage. His eyes were wide, his face flushed and his normally coiffured hair flew around his head making him look like something from the Rocky Horror Show.

'You bastard!' He yelled at Kell, pulling the gun out of the waist band of his trousers as he crossed the room to where Kell was immobilised. Dulac raised the gun over his head and brought it down with crack on the side of his skull.

Kell saw stars and felt the blood oozing down his scalp and onto his cheek.

'You think you can get one over on Bobby Dulac and get away with it!' He swung the gun at Kell's head but the sudden shifting of the boat at speed made him lose his balance and miss, his momentum making him stumble across the cabin. The intercom buzzed; Dulac steadied himself against the wall picked it up and listened. 'Ok, do it.'

The boat changed direction, veering sharply to starboard and started to slowly reduce speed. Dulac turned to Blondie who had watched Dulac's assault on Kell impassively. 'Get the outboard ready. We're going to ditch this beast and head to shore.' As Blondie went to carry out his orders, Dulac looked at Kell and said, 'It's just a case of whether we take you with us as insurance or you join your friend Henry at the bottom of the river.'

'Target is reducing speed and bearing starboard. It looks like they are heading to shore on the south bank of the river,' Charlie Smith yelled above the sound of the wind and the river as they barrelled in pursuit of Sophie's Dream.

John Dean turned to Packham, 'Looks like they're heading to shore. It's too shallow for a boat of their size to land anywhere. So they'll be using a small outboard from about 50 meters out. We can get closer to shore and will have to do the same. All in all, this is good as we'll be right behind them by the time they reach shore. Unless they've got a car waiting, then bingo, we've got them.' Dean radioed the update to the Counter Terrorism Unit and the Tilbury boat and gave the instruction to prepare the small inflatable for launch.

Through the binoculars, Packham could see Sophie's Dream heading for the south bank of the river. The Dartford crossing loomed in the background, crushed by the never ending weight of traffic that moved slowly across it every second of every day. He turned to Dean, 'That's the Littlebrook Power Station isn't it?'

'Yeh. It's in the process of being decommissioned. It provides decent access to the M25 but I don't think this was part of their plan. I doubt they'll have a car, so it should be game over.'

Blondie released Kell from the chair and immediately retied his hands behind his back. He led him up to the main deck where the boat had slowed in preparation of the launch of the outboard. He looked up river and saw the police launch speeding towards them.

Dulac was already in the outboard as Blondie pushed Kell toward the steps where he climbed down and sat opposite the American. Blondie released the rope and jumped down to join them. As he was in mid-air, the larger vessel turned hard to port and sped away down river.

It was less than a hundred metres to shore which gave Kell about a minute to make his decision.

'Stay with the outboard, Charlie. I'll get the Tilbury boat to intercept Sophie's Dream.' Dean barked the instructions over the radio as the welcome sound of the helicopter roared overhead.

As the CTU chopper flew overhead, Dulac fired a couple of shots neither of which came close to their target but did force the chopper to arc away to a safer distance. With Dulac distracted by the shooting, Kell leant back over the side of the outboard until gravity took over and he plunged into the murky waters of the River Thames. He twisted and turned, kicking as hard as he could to get his head up towards the surface and then kicked again to start a tortuous climb to the surface. Weighted down by his clothes and unable to use his arms, the ascent was agonising. His lungs were burning as he desperately held his breath. He could see the light of the surface and made frantic kicks towards the lifesaving oxygen. As if his body was on autopilot, he took a breath a split second before he hit the surface. His lungs filled with the filthy water and Justin Kell's world went black.

'Christ, Justin has fallen into the river! Slow down so I can go and help him.' Packham yelled at Dean.

'Charlie, take their boat out. Ram it if you have to and then turn back to where Kell entered the water. Chris, it'll just take a matter of seconds to put them in the water and then we'll pick up Justin.'

They were less than twenty meters from their prey as Charlie Jones swung the RIB hard to port and sent its bow wave crashing over Dulac and Blondie. For good measure, the stern of the police vessel glanced the side of the smaller boat which sent it spinning into the air depositing the occupants into the water.

Within seconds, the RIB was circling around the spot where Kell entered the river. Packham took off his life jacket and shoes and dived into the murky water.

'Anything on the sonar?' Dean asked Smith

'The water's too shallow and there's so much debris on the bottom that it's difficult to be certain.'

They watched Packham disappear beneath the surface and waited.

The moment Justin Kell swallowed a mouthful of the filthy water, he blanked out. The many times before when this had happened had put his life at risk. This time it saved it.

His mind took over and he held his breath, removing the urgent need to breath and numbing the pain of water already taken into his lungs. He kicked and kicked his legs, the agonising pain in his muscles just a mere dull ache. He broke the surface at the same time as Packham, who was gulping in air in preparation for his next dive.

'There he is!' yelled Charlie Smith, as he manoeuvred the boat alongside Kell, who was now face down in the water. Packham swam across to help the crew as they hauled the body onto the boat. Dean didn't bother untying him. There wasn't time. He turned Kell onto his back, sat astride him and started to work with compressions on his chest. A moment later Kell's eyes shot open and he coughed a couple of mouthfuls of river water onto the deck.

Packham had climbed back onto the boat and stood looking down at his friend.

Kell smiled up at him, 'I didn't know you cared Chris.'

Sinking to his knees, Packham replied, 'Neither did I.'

The moment was lost as Smith kicked in the engines and turned the boat towards the shore. The helicopter had landed and armed police with automatic rifles were standing up the bank with their weapons pointing at two sorry looking figures stumbling out of the water.

'Keep your hands in the air. No sudden movements or we will shoot.'

As Dulac and Blondie got to the shoreline and started across the stony ground towards the grassy bank, the officer in charge shouted.

'On your knees, hands behind your head.'

As Dulac sank to his knees, his hand shot into the inside of his jacket where his gun was holstered. Before it came into view, the air was split with the crack of two shots as the CTU shot Bobby Dulac dead.

Chapter 36

Alfio Mignemi was charm itself as he entered the police station on Bishopsgate. He displayed the confidence of a man who didn't have a care in the world.

Strictly speaking, it was DI Chris Packham who was the arresting officer, but in his absence the young DS completed the booking in process, which was almost like checking into a hotel but without having to pay for the privilege. Shortly after this had been completed, Mignemi's solicitor arrived. He had been called from the police car and immediately demanded time alone with his client.

They were led to a secure interview area and waited for the door to be shut and locked before they spoke.

'Thank you for coming so quickly Miguel. I have a flight back to Beirut this evening, so I need you to work your magic.'

Miguel Santini was in his early sixties. A few years older than Mignemi and he looked it. A small man with hunched shoulders and a poor taste in suits, he was the antithesis of his friend who he had known since they met at university all those years ago. It was foolish however, to be taken in by his shabby almost downtrodden appearance. Miguel Santini was a brilliant lawyer. He shared the same employer as his client and was one of a small number of people that operated within the inner sanctum of the Lebanese mafia.

'What have they arrested you for and how legitimate is it?' Like Mignemi, Santini got straight to the point.

'The murder of the footballer in Chicago. We've had a reporter and ex-cop, sniffing around the Horizon operation. One of our employees, Henry Gray, has proved to be a weak link and I suspect their police are slowly putting two and two together. We have cleared everything out and Robert is taking care of the loose ends as we speak.'

Santini, pondered on his friend's summary of events before responding, 'There is clearly no evidence linking you to the crime, so they are just stalling, playing for time. Possibly because something bigger is pending. OK, let us talk to them and get you out of here.'

By the time they were ready to commence the formal interview, two Special Branch officers had arrived and joined the arresting DS in the interview room. The tape was switched on and introductions completed. Before the DS could detail the charge, Santini got on the front foot.

'Before we go any further, please can you outline the evidence you have that makes you conclude that my client has anything to do with this crime.'

Sticking to the protocol, the DS repeated the charge for the benefit of the tape but was interrupted by Santini repeating his demand for details of the evidence.

It was agreed with the Special Branch officers, that the arrest for the murder of JJ Carmichael would need to be played out in full. This would then lead to the money laundering link, which would enable them to move the questioning to the investigation they were pursuing. But this meant that the Carmichael murder charge had to appear reasonable.

Ignoring the lawyer's request for the evidence to be put on the table, the DS continued with questions about Mignemi's involvement with the Horizon Life Settlement fund and his relationship with Bobby Dulac. Despite Santini's irritation, the questions continued for a couple of hours before the DS called for a break.

Mignemi and his solicitor were shown back to the secure area, where tea and coffee were waiting.

'You won't be flying tonight, Alfio. I believe they will play out this charade until they feel justified in expanding their questioning. The inference of money laundering and links to organised crime are already being made. They can carry on like this for 72 hours when they will either charge you formally or let you go. We can still get you out of the country, but your freedom of movement will be somewhat restricted.'

Mignemi was reflective when he spoke, 'Then I need to hope our employers can be convinced of my value to their organisation.'

The door opened and a uniformed officer led them back to the interview room.

When they walked in, Mignemi recognised the man now sitting at the desk.

The tape was switched on and DI Christopher Packham spoke, 'Alfio Mignemi I am charging you with conspiracy to the murder of Henry Gray…' he continued with the Miranda rights and finished by saying, 'and we have all the evidence to ensure that you'll be going away for a very, very long time.'

Chapter 37

Kell and Packham stood on the bank of the river surveying the crime scene.

'He must have been desperate or just plain stupid to pull a gun on armed police officers. It shows what we are dealing with here. Whoever he's working for must be into some serious shit. Anyway, I've got to get back to see our friend Mignemi before he disappears.'

Packham walked over to the CO and told him they would head back on the police RIB. He had provided the details of their part in the incident and everyone would be required to give full statements later. But for now, there was still an active investigation going on.

They left the crime scene as Blondie was being put in the back of a police van. Back on the RIB, they were able to change into dry if not very flattering clothes.

They were sitting in the back of the boat as Packham turned to his friend. 'Why did you tip yourself into the river?'

'Dulac had lost it. He was like a raving mad man. They were taking me along as insurance but I knew he could shoot me at any moment. It was a split second decision but I knew it was my only chance.' Kell paused before continuing, 'Thanks by the way. For coming in after me.'

'You owe me one and I don't mean a second rate curry!'

They both laughed and then enjoyed the silence of their thoughts as they turned the evening's events over in their minds.

'Is your mobile working? Kell asked. 'Mine got retired to the bottom of the river.'

'Sure, it's in my jacket. I'll get it for you.' Packham rose and went up to the bridge where his jacket was a crumpled tangle in the corner of the floor.

'Just ten minutes to our Tower Bridge station.' said Charlie Jones.

Packham handed his phone to Kell. 'Assume it's Amy you're calling?'

'Yes, I need to make sure she's alright and warn her not to take any drinks from strangers. Damn it! Her number was in my phone and her business card in my wallet.' Kell was staring at the handset as if hoping for divine inspiration.

'Just google her firm.' Said Packham.

'It's nearly nine o'clock. There won't be anyone there. Damn it!'

'Calm down Justin. I'm sure she's just fine. With Dulac dead and Mignemi in custody there's no one to give the order. Call her in the morning.'

Kell was sure there had been mention of Amy whilst he was on Sophie's Dream. He was certain there had been talk about using the same drug that had debilitated Gray, but was the hit set in progress? It didn't matter as far as Horizon was concerned, but if the instruction had been given, then as per his friend's logic, there was no one to order it to be stopped.

The RIB docked at the Tower Bridge station. They expressed their thanks to Dean and his crew and walked onto the jetty. There was a car waiting for Packham to take him to the police station.

'Do you want a lift to the station Justin?'

'It's just as easy for me to get a cab from here, thanks.'

'If you can come to my office first thing in the morning, we can take your statement then. Now go home, have a hot shower and get some sleep.' Packham got in the car and Kell watched as it sped away. As he walked up to Lower Thames Street to hail a cab, he couldn't stop worrying about Amy.

Despite the trauma of the evening's events and his concerns over Amy, Justin Kell slept like a log. He followed his friend's advice to the letter and as soon as his head hit the pillow, he was asleep.

On his way to meet Packham the next morning he called into the Apple store in Covent Garden and went through the rigmarole of getting a new phone and checking that all his contacts had been successfully downloaded from the Cloud. The first call on his new phone was to Amy's office. Much to his relief, he was told that she was in the office but busy in meetings all day. And yes, the receptionist would ask her to ring him as soon as she was free. And yes, she understood that it was very important.

It was gone 11.00 by the time he reached the Met's HQ on Victoria Embankment. 'So this is first thing, is it? What an easy life you journalists have.' Despite the sarcastic tone, Packham smiled as he greeted his friend with a man hug.

'Needed to get a new phone. I'm lucky to be here now with all the crap you have to go through just to prove who you are! Anyway, Amy's ok. She's in the office and will call me when she's free. Once I'm done here, I'm going to head north and spend the rest of the week up there.'

'It must be love,' joked Packham. 'Come on let's get this thing over with.'

Providing the statement took a lot longer than Kell had expected. They went right back to the death of Mike Jones and then every detail of the events leading up to the boat chase of the previous day. They sent out for a sandwich lunch and were regularly supplied with coffee. It was all recorded with a transcript taken at the same time. It was three o'clock before it was finished.

'Thanks for that Justin. You'll be called as a witness when Mignemi and Llubov, aka Blondie to you, go to trial. I'll let you know if we need anything else.'

On his way out of the building, Kell listened to his messages. One was from Amy saying she was fine but very busy and would ring him later when she got home from the gym.

Justin Kell froze as all the pieces slowly fell into place.

The quickest way to get to Euston was by tube. He headed for Embankment and jumped onto the Northern Line. It was a race against time if what he suspected was true. The next train to Manchester was at 15.50, arriving into Manchester Piccadilly at 18.00 if there were no delays. Once he was settled into the first class carriage, he rang Packham and was relieved when he picked up on the first ring.

'Justin, is everything ok?'

He relayed his concerns about Amy's recently acquired gym buddy but couldn't remember her name.

Having witnessed the lengths that Mignemi and Dulac would go to, Packham concluded there was credence in his friend's theory. 'OK Justin, I'll get a uniform to meet you at the station and you can go and pick Amy up. I'll text you the details when it's confirmed. In the meantime, if you get through to Amy tell her to go to the local police station and get them to call me.'

'Thanks Chris,' Kell ended the call and rang Amy's mobile. He left her the first of what would be six messages.

Chapter 38

Darya Llubov was not unduly concerned when her brother had not called her with an update on progress with operation Horizon. He was regularly out of contact, sometimes for up to a couple of weeks, depending on what orders he got from Mignemi. She had her instructions that the termination of Amy Speight had to take place by the end of the week and she was going to complete them as she always did. She took great pride in the fact that she had never let the organisation down. She had a 100% record and she intended to keep it that way. Along with her brother, they had a growing reputation in the world of organised crime and they were starting to reap the rewards for their reliability in completing whatever they were asked.

She had agreed to meet Speight at their gym in Bramhall. She planned to do a weight session before embarking on a ten mile run as per the schedule, in their preparation for the half marathon. She had already given Speight a couple of bottles of the new isotonic drink and was satisfied that its effects were slowly beginning to show. *The stupid cow thought her lethargy and nagging headaches were due to her hectic work life. Little did the bitch know that if all went to plan, she wouldn't have to worry about getting the miles into her legs after this evening.* By the end of the evening she would be dead.

Speight's 5.30 meeting overran. It was quarter past six by the time she'd wrapped things up and hurried out of the office to her car. She was meeting Darya at 6.30 and it was starting to get embarrassing that she was always turning up late. She'd put her phones on silent earlier that afternoon and with back to back meetings, had forgotten to unmute them. She was therefore blissfully ignorant of the frantic messages her new love had left her and that she was literally running towards her death.

'Sorry, I'm a bit late Darya. My last meeting overran.'

'No problem, I've only just got here myself. Come on, let's go and get changed. I thought we could do some weights and stretching and then do our ten mile route out towards Lyme Park.'

'I'm not sure I can manage ten miles,' replied Speight. 'I'm still not feeling 100% and can't shake off this nagging headache.'

'The fresh air will clear your head. Anyway, if you're struggling, we can cut it short,' Llubov smiled as she followed Speight into the changing room. 'Here, I got some more of that isotonic drink we've been trying. I find it really helps, especially when running.' She passed Amy a bottle as they walked into the ladies' section of the gym which as usual was deserted on a Wednesday evening at 7.00 pm.

It was a muggy early summer evening as they started with their stretches and warm up routine, before Llubov led them through their circuit. As the session progressed, the more and more Amy Speight drank. When they finished, she collapsed against the wall, sweating profusely and gasping for breath.

'I don't think I can do a run tonight Darya. I'm absolutely knackered.'

Llubov smiled, 'Don't worry. You won't be running anywhere.'

Time seemed to be moving in slow motion for Justin Kell as the Virgin Train sped along the West Coast mainline towards Manchester. There had been various calls with Packham who had arranged for a car to meet Kell at Piccadilly and the local force had been requested to confirm the details of the gym that Amy Speight was a member of. The train made its penultimate stop at Stockport. Kell was blissfully unaware that Stockport was a lot nearer to Bramhall than Manchester Piccadilly station. More importantly, the local police who had the details of Speight's gym, didn't put two and two together correctly either.

As soon as the train doors were unlocked, Kell ran down the platform and followed the signs to the Fairfield Street exit. The police car was waiting in the no parking tow-away zone and Kell jumped into the back seat. Following brief introductions, he asked, 'has Amy gone to any of the local police stations?'

The sergeant in the driver's seat replied, 'No, not yet. All of the stations in Greater Manchester area have been notified to call us if she appears. We've confirmed that Miss Speight is a member of the Liberty Gym in Bramhall, Stockport. I assume that's where you would like us to head? It should take about thirty minutes to get there.'

'Christ, my train stopped at Stockport. You should have met me there! Didn't you guys think!' Kell slammed his hand against the back of the seat in front of him.'

'We were instructed to meet you here, sir.' The tone in the sergeant's voice made it clear he understood they'd missed a trick.

Kell looked at his watch. It was just gone twenty past six. Providing there were no issues with traffic, they would get to the gym about ten to seven. But would they be too late?

Darya Llubov opened her locker and pulled out her back pack. Inside was a small sealed bottle and a syringe in its vacuum packed wrapper. She extracted the syringe and pushed it into the clear liquid inside the bottle. When it was nearly full, she extracted the needle, held the syringe up to the light and gently pressed the plunger until a couple of drops squirted from the tip. She put on her bum bag which she always wore when running and carefully put the syringe inside. She put the bottle into her back pack together with the tracksuit top she had taken off. The locker was empty. She didn't intend to hang around once the deed had been done.

Amy Speight took another gulp of her drink. She picked up the Lancome Soap Bag that she kept the bits and pieces in that she always took to the gym. Lip salve, tissues and her phone. She felt so terrible she thought of ringing an ambulance. She unlocked her phone and saw she had seven missed calls from Justin and three voicemails. She tapped the first voicemail message, put the phone to her ear and heard the frantic voice of her new boyfriend.

'Amy, listen very carefully. Whatever you're doing, wherever you are, go straight to the nearest police station and ask them to call Detective Inspector Chris Packham at the Met. You are in grave danger. I can't remember her name, but you must keep away from that friend of yours you met at the gym. She is trying to kill you by poisoning your drinks. Please Amy, I am

serious. Go to the local police station and I'll meet you there later this evening. I love you.'

She looked in horror at the drink she had just put down. Darya, surely not? She looked around the room frantically looking for something to defend herself with. She looked at the double doors expecting Darya to reappear at any moment. The gym floor had the usual array of abandoned weights, balance balls and mats. Her eyes caught a weight bar lying near the double doors that were the only entrance to the room. The doors opened inwards, each with a pull handle. If she could just put the weight bar through the pull handles, it might just buy her a couple of minutes so she could call for help. The adrenalin kicked in and she staggered to the weight bar. It was about four feet in length and still had what looked like a five kilo weight secured to one end. She managed to drag it to the door and then from somewhere deep down, managed to lift it and push the weight free end through the pull handles. She collapsed against the wall, just as she heard footsteps coming down the corridor towards her. She had just started to scramble back to her phone when she heard the doors push against her make shift barrier.

The traffic getting out of the city centre was heavy, even with the blues and twos blaring and flashing, the police car was regularly having to stop or weave in and out between cars and trams. When they eventually hit Princes Road, they were able to make much quicker progress.

'The gym is one of those automated places with no reception area. You need a swipe card and a code to gain entry. HQ is trying the out of hour's number but there's no reply. If there's no one about, we'll have to break in,' the sergeant spoke as they swung off the M60 onto the A34. 'Should be there in approximately ten minutes.'

Not expecting any resistance in the doors, Llubov banged her knee when they didn't open as expected. 'Ah, what have we got here? Amy, what do you think you're doing?'

Fumbling with her phone, trying to dial 999, Amy screamed back, 'Keep away from me you bitch. The police are on their way. Just fuck off out of my life.'

'Now, now Amy, watch your language.' Llubov pushed at the doors which opened about twelve inches. She could see Amy on the other side of the room, desperately tapping on her phone. 'I don't think the police are coming are they Amy, otherwise you wouldn't still be trying to call them.' She pushed at the doors again and they opened a little bit more as the weight bar began to slip to one side. A couple more hard shoves and the weighted end fell away and Darya Llubov walked over to her prey extracting the syringe from her bum bag on the way.

Llubov kicked Amy in the head. The kick came with such speed that Amy didn't see it coming. The phone fell from her hand as the operator said, 'Emergency services, which service do you require?'

Llubov straddled Amy's body, checked the syringe and leaned down to administer its deadly poison.

Desperately trying to resist, Amy's right hand grasped a small two kilo dumbbell. Just as she felt the needle break her skin, she swung it with the last amount of energy she had left, into the skull of her erstwhile gym buddy. Llubov went sprawling and the syringe flew out of her hand. Amy collapsed into unconsciousness just as Kell, followed by two police officers burst into the room.

Epilogue

Six Months Later

Justin Kell walked out of the offices of the Fund Management Journal for the last time. In the end, the decision had been an easy one. His inside track reporting of the Horizon Settlement Fund scandal had gone global. He'd written articles for the full range of industry publications and also for the financial sections of the serious tabloids and the FT. With the trial of Mignemi and the Llubov siblings due to start in a few weeks, he was required to stick to the core elements of the story, principally the demise of a financial institution and how the regulatory system had failed to identify such serious malpractice resulting in thousands of investors losing their money. He was allowed to reference the suspicious death of Henry Gray but as this was one of the charges in the upcoming trial, he could not include any details.

He had signed an agreement with a large publishing house to write a serialisation of the story once the legal proceedings were concluded but this was likely to be twelve months away. Despite offers to join the editorial staff at various national and international news desks, including the BBC, he decided that he wanted the freedom of being freelance. He wanted to write about the truth. To investigate and write stories that made a difference. That exposed the evil in the world and to help right the wrongs that the mass population never even heard about.

Initially, Amy thought he was too idealistic. But as they recounted the horrific events of six months ago, over and over, she eventually understood that it wasn't just the story that motivated Kell but ensuring the truth was told and justice served.

Amy spent just over a week in hospital after the attack by Darya Llubov. Fortunately, the hypodermic had only scratched her. A few days on a saline drip to rehydrate her and umpteen tests to ensure there was no permanent damage was all it took before she got back to everyday life. The worst of it was not how close she'd come to death but how stupid she'd been to trust this woman who just appeared in her life out of nowhere. She insisted on returning to work immediately despite Justin's and her boss' protests. She wanted everything to return to normal as soon as possible.

Amy and Justin were well aware of the theory that relationships formed out of extreme stress, survivor - saviour situations were not supposed to last, but in the weeks following the attempt on her life, they had become inseparable.

Her boss was fully supportive of her moving to London. They would maintain the Manchester office and Amy would still get up there every couple of weeks, but the action was in the capital and Amy would be more effective with this as her base. Kell gave notice on the flat he rented in Leytonstone and they rented in Victoria before deciding where to buy.

The assignment of her life policy to the defunct Horizon, did not go through. Amy often smiled to herself when she thought of this being a good deal; her life instead of £250k she would never have got to spend.

Amy was already home when Kell opened the door of the first floor flat on the corner of Ebury Street.

'Hi, how did it go?'

Kell smiled, 'It went just fine. Would you believe that they bought me a pen as a leaving present!'

'Very imaginative,' said Amy as she walked across the room and gave him a big hug.

'It is a Mont Blanc and they did get it engraved, so I'm not complaining.'

Kell sat on the sofa and Amy disappeared into the kitchen and returned with a bottle of Verve and two glasses.

'What are we celebrating?' asked Kell.

'Us stupid! And your new job.' Amy opened the bottle and poured the fizz.

'Cheers,' they both said at the same time as they chinked glasses.

'In case you hadn't realised, I'm now self-employed and don't actually have any stories or articles in the pipeline. So I'm going to be a kept man for a little while.'

Amy leant over and gave him a kiss, 'Fine with me. So long as I keep you for a very long time. Any news on the trial?'

'I did speak to Chris earlier. It will probably start next month. Blondie is charged with the murder of Henry and his charming sister with your attempted murder. Our evidence will be critical in convicting them but they'll be going away for a very long time.'

'What about Mignemi?' asked Amy.

'There is nothing that directly links him to the Horizon operation or the countless murders in the US including the footballer. He wasn't on the boat when Henry died and whilst it is clear to me and the police that he was the top man, he's saying it was all Dulac and doesn't know anything about anything. The enquiries into his links with organised crime have come to nothing. He's charged with conspiracy to murder Henry, but the odds are, he'll walk.'

They finished their drinks and Amy said, 'Come on, let's go out and get something to eat. I can tell you all about my day and a beautiful house I've found down in Esher. We can save the rest of the bottle for when I hear if they've accepted the offer I put in.'

Justin Kell smiled as he put his coat back on and walked out into a cold London evening.

THE END